William Winter, William John Hennessy, William James Linton

Edwin Booth

In Twelve Dramatic Characters

William Winter, William John Hennessy, William James Linton

Edwin Booth
In Twelve Dramatic Characters

ISBN/EAN: 9783337375799

Printed in Europe, USA, Canada, Australia, Japan

Cover: Foto ©Andreas Hilbeck / pixelio.de

More available books at **www.hansebooks.com**

EDWIN BOOTH

IN

TWELVE DRAMATIC CHARACTERS.

THE PORTRAITS BY W. J. HENNESSY.

THE ENGRAVING BY W. J. LINTON.

THE BIOGRAPHICAL SKETCH BY WILLIAM WINTER.

BOSTON:

JAMES R. OSGOOD & COMPANY,

LATE TICKNOR & FIELDS, AND FIELDS, OSGOOD & Co.

1872.

ORDER OF ILLUSTRATIONS.

Drawn by *W. J. HENNESSY.* — Engraved by *W. J. LINTON.*

SKETCH OF EDWIN BOOTH.

"The purpose of playing, whose end, both at the first, and now, was, and is, to hold, as 't were, the mirror up to nature; to show virtue her own feature, scorn her own image, and the very age and body of the time his form and pressure."

— *Hamlet. Act* iii. *Scene* ii.

"We hear Shakspeare's men and women discussed, praised, liked, disliked, as real human beings; and in forming our opinions of them we are influenced by our own characters habits of thought, prejudices, feelings, impulses, just as we are influenced with regard to our acquaintances and associates."

— *Mrs. Jameson's " Characteristics of Women."*

"Thou gav'st me Nature as a kingdom grand,
With power to feel and to enjoy it. Thou
Not only cold, amazed acquaintance yield'st,
But grantest that in her profoundest breast
I gaze, as in the bosom of a friend.
The ranks of living creatures thou dost lead
Before me, teaching me to know my brothers
In air, and water, and the silent wood."

— *Goethe's Faust. Scene* xiv. — *Bayard Taylor's Translation.*

"Unmoved, though witlings sneer and rivals rail;
Studious to please, yet not ashamed to fail;
He scorns the meek address, the suppliant strain,
With merit needless, and without it vain.
In reason, nature, truth he dares to trust:
Ye fops be silent, and ye wits be just!"

— *Dr. Johnson — Prologue to " Irene."*

" Earthly fame
Is fortune's frail dependant; yet there lives
A Judge, who, as man claims by merit, gives:
To whose all-pondering mind a noble aim,
Faithfully kept, is as a noble deed;
In whose pure sight all virtue doth succeed."

— *Wordsworth's Sonnets.*

EDWIN BOOTH.

A BIOGRAPHICAL SKETCH, BY WILLIAM WINTER.

O BVIOUS difficulties perplex the biographer of a man still living. The in-completeness of an unfinished career necessarily precludes thoroughness and precision of estimate. Delicacy, at the same time, enjoins a careful reserve in the use of materials. Judgment is hampered, and choice is restricted. Details that would be entitled to conspicuous prominence, had the drama of life been acted out to its completion, must, since it is still going on, be greatly subordinated or altogether suppressed. The garland of praise that might fittingly be laid on a tomb-stone, cannot be laid on a library table. In this sketch of Edwin Booth, therefore, it will be the aim of the writer — glad in the happy obstacle which constrains him to reticence and brevity — simply to recount, in unembellished nar-rative, the principal facts of the actor's personal and professional career, and therewith to couple some general observations on his genius and his acting. The reader, it is hoped, will be content with authenticity in the sketch, and sincerity in the critical study.

Edwin Booth was born in Baltimore, in Maryland, on the 15th of November, 1833, being the fourth son of Junius Brutus Booth. His father was then thirty-seven years of age; had been seventeen years an actor; and was in the meridian of his life, his greatness, and his fame. Between him and this boy there existed, from the first, a profound and fervent, though silent and undemonstrative sympathy. As Edwin grew up, his close companionship seemed more and more to be needed and desired by the parent; and so it happened that he was frequently taken from school to accompany his father on professional expeditions. The educational training that he received was, therefore — as will be surmised — fitful and superficial. Ex-perience of the actual world, however — and, sometimes, very rough experience — combined with this irregular schooling, to develop his mind and mature his character. As a boy, he is represented to have been grave beyond his years — observant, thoughtful, and rather melancholy; but wise in knowledge of his surroundings, and strong in reticence and self-poise. He was accustomed to accompany his father as attendant and dresser; but, in fact, he was the chosen monitor and guardian of that wild genius, and possessed more influence over him than was exercised by any other person. This association, operating upon hereditary talent, wrought its inevitable consequence, in making Edwin Booth an actor. The strange life that he saw and led — a life in which fictitious emotions, imaginative influences, and every-day trivialities are so singularly blended — exerted its customary charm upon a youthful, sensitive, impressible nature, at once luring him toward the stage, and preparing him for its profession. His immediate entrance to a theatric career, however, was made precipitately, and in an accidental manner.

It took place at the Boston Museum, on the 10th of September, 1849. The elder Booth was then fulfilling an engagement there — the last but one that he played in Boston — and Edwin was, as usual, in attendance on his father. "Richard III." had been cast, and the player to whom the minor part of *Tyrrel* was allotted, desirous to be out of the bill, persuaded Edwin to relieve him of the duty. The arrangement was effected without consultation with the tragedian, nor did he learn, till a short time prior to the announced performance, that his son designed to appear: and he did not approve of the movement, when he thus became aware of it. From the first, indeed, and for a long time, the father opposed — though passively — his son's adoption of the dramatic calling. Nevertheless, Edwin drifted into it, and persevered in its pursuit. The Museum appearance attracted, of course, only a momentary attention. It was something for a youngster to have got on the stage and off again, without actually breaking down; but it was not much. This effort, though, was speedily followed by more ambitious attempts. At Providence, in the same season — and still in his father's train — the youthful aspirant acted *Cassio*, in "Othello," and *Wilford*, in "The Iron Chest" — his personation of the latter part being accounted a singularly meritorious and promising work. At the Arch Street Theatre, in Philadelphia, then conducted by Mr. E. S. Connor, his *Wilford*, in particular, met with emphatic approbation. Another of his juvenile successes, in which thoughtful observers discerned the germs of future excellence, was his *Titus*, in John Howard Payne's tragedy of "Brutus." Once, in the City of Washington, when the elder Booth acted the lion-hearted hero of this tragedy, Payne himself was present in the theatre, and Edwin's *Titus* — an incidental feature of the representation — won the approval of the author.

For more than two years, in a desultory, intermittent manner, acting with his father in various cities of the North and East, the novice continued to progress. Very little, of interest, however, is to be recorded with reference to this nebulous period of the actor's career. His first appearance on the New York stage was made at this time, as also was his first essay in the character of *Richard III.*, in which he was destined to win brilliant distinction. The first of these events took place on the 27th of September, 1850, at the National Theatre, in Chatham Street, when Edwin played *Wilford*, to the *Sir Edward Mortimer* of his father. The second occurred at the same theatre in 1851, when — at his father's instance, and on the night appointed for his father's benefit, with but brief notice and the scantiest preparation — he acted *Richard*. The *Richmond* was Mr. John R. Scott. Illness was assigned by the elder Booth as the cause of his non-appearance; but it was surmised that the illness was, in fact, feigned, for the purpose of putting Edwin's talents to a severe practical test. It proved a fortunate expedient, for it brought him both public interest and professional sympathy and encouragement. At the beginning of the performance, indeed, the audience, which was very numerous — received the new *Richard* doubtfully. No announcement had been made of a change in the cast, and no preliminary explanation was afforded to the spectators. Hastily conceived, and rendered possible by a concurrence of accidents, the movement was carried through with not unnatural precipitation. While the young actor was putting on the garb of the *Duke of Gloster*, a friend stood by, holding the play-book, and hearing his recital of the words of the part, to be certain that he possessed the text, and to refresh his memory wherever it should be at fault. Not till Edwin stood upon the stage, and the wild and joyous applause designed for his father had abruptly changed into dead silence, did the full gravity of the situation appear. The vast concourse of spectators had assembled to see their favorite tragedian, in his greatest character; and they might well have been astonished and annoyed at sight of the stripling in place of the giant. Their behavior, however, was exceedingly considerate and generous. As the performance proceeded, and grew in vigor, and the identity of the actor became manifest, pleasure succeeded surprise, and honest approval rewarded a worthy and daring effort. Edwin was called before the curtain, at the end of the play, and Mr. Scott, who led him forward, responded to the public greeting, and spoke the natural and sincere gratitude of the adventurous performer. It may be added that the theatre-going people of New York have had no reason to regret the favor which was then kindly bestowed on an unknown aspirant for recognition and cheering applause.

These were the first steps. It was in California, though, that the hard work of Edwin Booth's early professional career was performed, and that his first substantial successes were achieved. His elder brother, Junius — now the manager of the Boston Theatre, a gentleman equally esteemed for genial humor, practical sagacity, and energetic administrative talent for the business of public amusement —

had visited California, and returning thence, had brought rosy and alluring accounts of the prosperity there prevalent, and the opportunities there afforded for the rapid acquisition of wealth. It was his conviction that his father ought instantly to proceed to that Eldorado; and this belief he lost no opportunity of urging. The scheme did not commend itself to the immediate favor of the tragedian.

When free from the baleful influence of that insanity which lurked in his noble mind and sometimes afflicted it so grievously — driving him into dreadful and deplorable excesses — Booth was a man of sweet temperament and fine culture, sympathetic with whatever is best of delicacy, dignity, and refinement in old civilization, and necessarily averse, therefore, to contact with the asperities incidental to a new state of society. Hence, doubtless, the apprehensive solicitude with which he shrunk from the new, turbulent, untried region of labor thus opened before him. Another and a darker presentiment may have mingled with this feeling. The event proved his misgivings to be rational, when, at length, he had journeyed to the Golden Gate. This was in July, 1852. He had designed, at first, to leave Edwin at home, on the family farm, near Baltimore; and, in fact, he set out on the journey without him; but, after a little time, he stopped and sent back for his boy, and together they went on to San Francisco. His stay in California covered a period of three months. His opening engagement in the capital lasted two weeks and a half; was played at the Jenny Lind Theatre; and was equally remunerative in reputation and profit. Edwin and Junius were included in the stock company. From San Francisco the party proceeded to Sacramento; but there the enterprise failed — all the money that had been earned in the one place being lost in the other. One incident of this experience possesses a somewhat singular interest now, and therefore deserves to be recorded.

During their stay at Sacramento, the father and sons took each a benefit. For that of Edwin, Otway's "Venice Preserved" was represented, the elder Booth playing *Pierre*, and the younger playing *Jaffier*. It had long been, and still is, the irrational stage custom to dress *Jaffier* in a black velvet tunic, and corresponding trappings, not dissimilar in effect from the garb that is ordinarily worn by *Hamlet*. Seeing Edwin in this dress, his father — frequently, in those days, overtaken by that solemn, moody revery which often presages impending death — looked at him for a long time, curiously and sadly, and at last said: "You *look* like *Hamlet*. Why don't you play it?" "Perhaps I may, sometime," the young actor answered, "if I should ever have another benefit." This scene and these words came vividly back upon his memory, in after days, when the opportunity arose for him to play *Hamlet*, and, when in exact fulfillment of this implied pledge to his dead and gone father, he acted the part which has been the chief means of his development, his fortune, his fame, and the genuine, permanent, and loving esteem in which he is held by the great body of his countrymen.

In October, 1852, Booth bade farewell to his sons, and set out on his homeward journey. Before parting with Edwin — whom he had at length determined to leave to the pursuit of fortune — he spoke with him very gravely, and pointed out to him the advantages of learning the profession of acting, in a new country, and amid circumstances of comparative independence. The parting, on both sides, was difficult and melancholy; but there is no doubt that it was made in wisdom. Left to himself, the young actor would, inevitably, plunge into the toil of his arduous pursuit, with greater freedom and with better chances of success than when constrained beneath the constant observation of his parent and — in the public mind — overshadowed by the greatness of the abler and more famous artist. There comes a time in every young man's life when he must both learn and act for himself, and when, accordingly, the nearest and dearest friends and sagest counselors seem set apart from him. Experience cannot be imparted. It must be bought — and every human creature must pay its price. This time and this ordeal had now come for Edwin Booth, and the ordeal was to be very bitter. What befel his father, after leaving California, is well known to readers of dramatic biography; yet the mention of it should not be omitted here. He traveled in safety to New Orleans, and there filled an engagement — the last that he was destined to play — at the St. Charles's Theatre. It ended on the 19th of November, 1852, with his performance of *Sir Edward Mortimer* and *John Lump* — in the tragedy of "The Iron Chest," and the farce of "The Review." He then embarked on a Mississippi steamer, named the *J. S. Cheneworth*, for Cincinnati. At starting there was a shower of rain, and he got wet and took a cold. This he neglected, or only so far observed as presently to retire to his state-room and his bed. Here he lay, in silence and alone, for upwards of two days — worn out with the struggle of his own self-torturing spirit, with care, with labor, and with pain; but, to the last, reticent, patient, and unwilling to be a burden or annoyance to anyone. When found, he was in a dying condition. His death took place on the 30th of November, 1852, in the 57th year of his age. His grave is in the Baltimore Cemetery, near a monument erected to his memory by his son Edwin — who devoted to that filial duty the fruits of one of the first successful engagements that he played after returning to the East.

Much intervened before that return. The Californian period of Edwin Booth's career — inclusive of a trip to Australia and the Sandwich Islands — extended from the Summer of 1852 to the Autumn of 1856.   At first, after his father's departure, there was a brief period of waiting.   Then he got an engagement with Mr. D. W. Waller — now the stage-manager of Booth's Theatre, in New York — to act at Nevada and Grass Valley, playing all sorts of parts, in all sorts of pieces. Mr. Waller was the "star."   During this engagement Edwin played *Iago*, for the first time.

It proved an unfortunate engagement, though — attended by bad business, weary traveling, storms, and general discomfort, and terminating in absolute disaster. Hemmed in, at Grass Valley, by a snow storm more savage and overwhelming than its fellows, the wandering players, and, indeed, all the inhabitants of the place, were brought to the verge of starvation.   Days passed ; stores of food were well nigh expended ; and want and sorrow settled down upon this forlorn community.

Amid these distresses, an adventurous express-carrier, bursting through the snow, arrived with letters from the outer world, and one of these bore to Edwin Booth the grievous and dismal tidings of his father's death.   It came at night. The actor was absent from his lodgings, and had to be sought for by a comrade, whose face, on finding him, told — before a word was spoken — the whole black news of bereavement and affliction.   " My father is dead ! " cried Edwin.   " He is dead," returned the other, " and there is a letter for you at the tavern."

The whole town knew what had happened, and pitied the poor youth in his grief and desolation.   It was his first experience of great trouble, and the anguish it induced was rendered almost maddening by the thought that he had suffered his father to depart alone.   Anxiety as to his mother's welfare mingled with this emotion and augmented its bitterness.   He was nearly destitute of money ; far from home ; snow-bound in the wilderness ; and almost crazed with grief for the loss of the one being whom he loved best in the world.   Words are unnecessary to depict the gloom of this situation.   It was one that human reason could not endure with patience, nor long endure at all.

How to get to San Francisco, to his brother Junius, was now Booth's problem. There was no conveyance out of Grass Valley.   The nearest town was Marysville, fifty miles away.   The snow lay thick and heavy on all the roads.   In this desperate dilemma, Booth chanced to overhear the talk of a group of men, at a street corner, who spoke of their design to walk out of the town, rather than stay there and starve.   The men were rough, and their project was full of fearful peril : but the plan they announced opened the sole road of deliverance, and the actor instantly joined his fortunes with those of the daring strangers.   Each man contributed what he could to the common purse and larder ; a chief was chosen ; and the expedition set forth. Their journey to Marysville consumed two days and one night. Part of the night they rested in a wayside tavern. Often they were floundering in snow-drifts to their waists. Cold, hungry, tattered, and wretched, they reached their journey's end, and scattered to their several destinations.

Booth, now penniless, borrowed enough of money to pay for his passage to Sacramento, and thence to San Francisco, where he arrived in a condition that is mildly described as destitute, forlorn, and lamentable. His brother Junius, he found, had received later intelligence from home. Their father's body, this assured them, had reached Baltimore and been laid in the grave. Their mother's wants were neither many nor pressing. If they saw any prospect of good fortune in California, they would do wisely to remain there. They were not to return, at any sacrifice, on her account. This was the tenor of advice from the East, and by this they determined to abide.

Edwin Booth now became a member of a dramatic company, under his brother's management, to play "utility parts," at a little theatre called the San Francisco Hall. Farces and burlesques were done in abundance at this place, and in all of these the ready and versatile player took an active share. One of his hits, at this time, was made as *Dandy Cox*, in a negro farce, produced by a troupe known as the Chapman Family. Another was his personation of *Plume*, a local celebrity, one of those unfortunate creatures, common in all places, to whom notoriety, even though it involve ridicule, is the breath of life. Plume was reproduced in a farce, and so well reproduced, that his "counterfeit presentment" proved both popular and remunerative. Plume himself was pleased to signify approval; and he showed the sincerity of his satisfaction by sending to the actor his hat, coat, and gaiters. A more important success was made by Booth, at the same time, in Shakspeare's *Petruchio*, which he then first acted, and which he still retains in his repertory of acting parts.

Step by step, in this little theatre, he worked his way upward to better things. The work was hard, the discipline irksome, the drudgery various and incessant; but all this was valuable experience.

One night, for the benefit of a comrade, a member of the dramatic company whom he liked and wished to stead, he acted *Richard III.* The resultant success was truly magical. The city rang with his praises. Even the sensible and phlegmatic Junius was surprised and delighted at this outburst of tragic power: so much so, indeed, that he straightway advised his brother's appearance in a succession of the great characters of Shakspeare. Most of these Booth had studied. Many of them he has seen acted by his father — from whom it was his privilege to learn, and to whose genius and artistic example he has been deeply indebted and is known to be reverently grateful.   He accepted the opportunity and he proved equal to it.   His *Richard* was followed by his *Shylock*, and this by his *Macbeth*.   The result was a popular excitement unprecedented in the dramatic life of California.   Crowded houses applauded him.   The generous but not always judicious enthusiasm of the Press encouraged and cheered him. The sympathy of brother actors stimulated him to fresh exertions.   In a word, he became the favorite of the theatre-going public, and made an impression on the stage of his time, which — though it was modified by subsequent events, and though it has been changed in character through the lapse of years — was deep, strong, true, and destined to endure.

Towards the close of this series of Shakspearean performances at the San Francisco Hall, he obtained a benefit; and it was now — mindful of his father's significant suggestion, and of the half-promise to which it had led — that he first acted the part of *Hamlet*.   It was the crowning success of his daring enterprise, and it brought the crowning honors.   Through all the lawless strength, diffused effort, inequality, and crudeness of the personation, thoughtful observers saw the informing power and fire of dramatic genius.   Much was written about it, and about the actor, and much that was written was foolish.   Happily, however, he was not devoid of judicious counsel, nor of the sense to accept and profit by it. Critical articles, contributed to one of the local newspapers, by Mr. F. C. Ewer — now a distinguished member of the New York clergy — afforded him, in particular, salutary suggestions and useful guidance.   His brother Junius, also, was wise and kind in warning him against the possible ill effects of extravagant praise, and the danger of his mistaking imitative cleverness and the exuberant power of youth for complete mastery of the great art of acting.   "You have had a wonderful success for a young man," said this sagacious friend, "but you have a great deal to learn."   And this sensible view of the subject Junius proceeded to enforce, in his capacity of manager, as soon as the hurly-burly over Booth's Shaksperean performances had subsided, by casting him again for comedy, farce, and burlesque parts, of the commonest description.

The lull was not slow to come, and then affairs went on in the old way — though only for a little while.   A new theatre, called the Metropolitan, was presently opened, in the vicinity of the San Francisco Hall, with Miss Catherine Sinclair (Mrs. Edwin Forrest) as manager, and Mr. James E. Murdock as the first "star." The new establishment — neat, handsome, well appointed, and managed by an intellectual and thoroughly accomplished gentlewoman — speedily captivated the popular fancy. Public attention was diverted from the old theatre; the business grew bad; the company dwindled away; the place was finally abandoned to negro minstrelsy; and Edwin Booth, finding himself once more in want of employment, determined to go to Australia.

This was in 1854. The Australian trip, including an episode of professional experience at the Sandwich Islands, occupied nine months. Booth was accompanied by Mr. D. C. Anderson and Miss Laura Keene; and it was arranged that these three were to constitute the nucleus of a company to act in Sydney, Melbourne, and wherever else the star of adventure should guide them. After embarking in the brig that was to convey them across the Pacific, Booth made the interesting discovery that the captain's wife, who had been an actress, and who was crazy, had conceived the design of affording professional support to his performances in Australia, and had, therefore, come on board, with all her stage habiliments. Likewise he learned that another actress, in the line of "heavies," and possessed of some standing on the San Francisco stage, had been moved by a similar inspiration on his behalf, and was also present, with the requisite luggage. This "concatenation," as may be surmised, was comically completed by the arrival of Miss Laura Keene, and the meeting of the three astonished and suspicious tragedy-queens, in the vessel's cabin. This grotesque incident proved an augury of many more, the whole trip being made up of ludicrous vicissitudes. These, however, were rendered tolerable by occasional blessings of prosperity. The voyage from San Francisco to Sydney consumed seventy-two days, during twelve of which the brig lay becalmed upon the Summer ocean.

Arrived at Sydney, the dramatic adventurers speedily found an opening. Booth made his first appearance as *Shylock*, and played a successful engagement. Then the party proceeded to Melbourne, where they were less fortunate, and where Booth's business relations with Miss Keene were terminated. Finally, the actor took passage for San Francisco, in a vessel that was to stop at the Sandwich Islands. Accompanied by Mr. Anderson, Mr. John Roe, and a few other players, he disembarked at Honolulu, hired the sole theatre in the town, and remained there two months — producing, among other plays, "Richard III." and "The Lady of Lyons." His companion, Mr. Roe, who possessed great skill in the delineation of female characters, acted *Pauline*. Most of the dramatic company, poverty continuing to prevail, slept in hammocks rigged up in the theatre. Booth himself went about and pasted his posters on the fences — not, indeed, to save expenses, but because he found that the native boys, whom he had employed to do this work, ate the paste (poy), and threw away the play-bills. A certain measure of prosperity rewarded the actor's enterprise — but not much — and he therefore presently concluded to push on to San Francisco.

On his arrival, Miss Catherine Sinclair offered him an engagement, at the Metropolitan Theatre, where, accordingly, he reappeared before the California public, playing, for the first time, *Benedick*, in "Much Ado about Nothing." At a later period, Booth and this lady formed a business partnership, to travel and act, which was distinguished, as to its results, by one incident of especial interest — the first production in America of the drama of " The Marble Heart." Miss Sinclair was the original *Marco;* Booth the original *Raphael;* and Mr. Henry Sedley the original *Volage.* The novelty, as of course it then was, met with "acceptance bounteous;" and its presentation, which took place at Sacramento, may certainly be of right recorded as the most important event of the dramatic season of 1855, in California.

The partnership soon came to an end, and Booth started on other wanderings. This time he journeyed from Sacramento into the adjacent mountains, with a strolling manager, named Moulton, who had organized a dramatic company, and provided a wagon for its transportation, as also a brass band to make music by the way. Booth traveled on horseback, with this distinguished cortege, halting now and then to act, and so making the mountain circuit. The expedition met with rather a fluctuating public favor, but was uniformly attended by one startling accompaniment. Each town took fire as soon as Mr. Moulton's cavalcade had left it; and so regularly did this lurid phenomenon recur, that at last it became the theme of general remark and speculation, and Booth was known and mentioned as " The Fiery Star." It was an epithet of ill-omen, but, as a warning, it served him well. Ignorant and lonely communities are readily superstitious and dangerously impulsive. There was no obvious link between the strollers and the conflagrations; but, somehow, the logic of the hardy mountaineers deduced the one from the other, and, as an obvious consequence, traveling became unsafe for Mr. Moulton's caravan. At Downingsville, Booth found such reason for solicitude with reference to his personal safety that he deemed it judicious to ride immediately out of the town. The discreet manager, having private reasons to dread the sheriff, followed this example. Indeed, he improved upon it — for he ran away, not only from Downingsville but from his company. The subsequent chaos may readily be imagined. The band ceased to blow; the actors dispersed; the driver of the wagon seized Booth's horse, as payment of the money owed to him by the manager; and, to every appearance, "the fiery star" was quenched. He still retained a few trinkets, though, and of these he made the best use. Hard-

ships had to be endured; but these were not new to him, and youth can endure
a great deal. Through much distress, and without a sixpence in his pocket, the
tragedian drifted back to Sacramento — tired enough, by this time, of painful
vicissitudes and unrequited toil. Thoughts of home, and longings for a more refined
field of labor were beginning to color his moods, and sway his purposes. He
wished, with all his heart, to return to the East. It was not long before the
wish became a purpose, and the purpose a possibility. In Sacramento he found
true friendship, urgent counsel towards the right road, and practical assistance.
Two benefit performances were arranged for him, in succession, and both were
successful — a result largely due to the heart and zeal of his friend, M. P. Butler,
who labored in his cause with devoted assiduity and the tact of true affection,
and thus aroused and stimulated the whole theatrical community to give him, at
parting, a substantial mark of admiration and good-will. A cheering crowd accompanied him to the river-side, and saw him safely embarked.

At San Francisco he was tendered another benefit, and once more exchanged a
farewell greeting with the California public. On this occasion, and for the first time,
he acted *King Lear.* His departure from California took place in September, 1856.

The narrative of Booth's professional experience from this time onward — relating, as it does, to a period of his life which has passed, for the most part,
in wide and full publicity — must touch on topics familiarly known, and, therefore,
may well assume a more condensed and rapid form of expression than has hitherto
been employed.

The roughest portion of the actor's experience was now over. Other troubles —
some of them the bitterest that man can know — were yet to be encountered;
but physical hardships and cares of a sordid kind were past, and the star of good
fortune began to loom, large and bright, above the horizon. Those friends in
California who had anticipated prosperity and fame for Edwin Booth in the older
States speedily found their best anticipations fulfilled. He came upon a play-
going community that was more than commonly eager for novelty. He came, also,
with the prestige of a renowned name — sufficient in itself to insure him an immediate and sympathetic hearing. And what he thus attracted he amply repaid.
All who saw him at this time saw a young man of extraordinary personal graces,
robust yet refined vigor, and a spirit magnetically bright and ardent with the fire
of youthful genius. In the form of his acting there were manifest defects, arising
partly from lack of culture and partly from lack of attrition with intellectual and
refined society; but the actor's art, the power to imagine and assume states of
emotion and phases of character, may exist, in admirable perfection, apart from the

self-knowledge and the serene graces that these bestow; and it was felt that in
the soul of Booth's acting there was spontaneous passion, imaginative power, and
the nameless beauty which thrills, entices, and ennobles, and which is the insepa-
rable and celestial attribute of inspiration.   The surprised and delighted public
recognized this charm, and met it with full and encouraging sympathy.

Booth made his first appearance, after coming to the Atlantic coast, at the
Front Street Theatre, Baltimore, and from that place — heralded by a joyous noise
of his own triumph — he made a rapid tour of the South and South-West,
playing successful engagements in all the large cities of that region.   Washington,
Richmond, Charleston, New Orleans, Mobile, and Memphis were among the capitals
that opened their arms to receive him, and in all of them he laid the foundations of
solid reputation, "whole as the marble, founded as the rock."

In Richmond he met for the first time the lady whom he was destined to wed.
The sweet and grave import of this incident in his experience will be understood,
without remark, by all readers for whom these words are intended.   At a later
point the gentle name of Mary Devlin will once more grace this sketch, which
here must not relinquish the direct thread of its story.

What Booth regarded as the most important of the series of performances by
which he was endeavoring to revive, in the Atlantic States, the memory and the lustre
of a great name, was now given at Boston.   The play-goers of that city were remarkable, in those days, for a refinement of taste and a severity of judgment which,
since then, appears to have fallen somewhat into decay.   The actor, accordingly,
looked forward to his appearance there with natural trepidation.   Should it prove a
failure, he was fully determined to subside into "the stock."   Should it prove a
success, he would press on to the fulfillment of more ambitious designs than he
had yet disclosed.   The result is well known.   Booth appeared at the Boston
Theatre, in April, 1857, in the character of *Sir Giles Overreach*, and at once attained
a brilliant triumph.   It was the turning-point of his career.   It banished self-
distrust; it confirmed him in a just and proper estimate of his own talents;
and it strengthened his resolve to attempt those magnificent enterprises, for the
advancement of the stage, which he has since pursued so steadfastly, and with
results so valuable to art in this nation.

From Boston, Booth proceeded to New York.   Injudicious and unauthorized
announcements had been promulgated, in advance of his coming — ostentatious and
absurd placards, put forth by an agent, which gave the public to understand that the
mantle of the famous father had fallen upon the son, and that "Richard was himself
again."   These ebullitions of mercantile and misguided enthusiasm caused the

tragedian a great deal of mortification, and, indeed, drove him into the folly of a fit of intemperance, which well-nigh proved the ruin of his engagement. He had intended to begin with *Sir Giles Overreach;* but, as *Richard III.* was promised, he kept faith with the public and appeared in that character. This was at Burton's Metropolitan Theatre, on the 14th of May, 1857. Mr. Joseph N. Ireland, in his copious and valuable "Records of the New York Stage" (which contain, however, but scant information on the subject of this sketch), says that Booth played *Richard*, on this occasion, "with a brilliancy and force that surpassed the warmest expectations of his friends," and that he "gave evidence of the highest order of talent, and created a sensation hitherto unequalled by any native-born actor, Forrest alone excepted."

During this engagement he acted a round of parts, including — besides *Richard III. — Sir Giles Overreach, Richelieu, Shylock, Lear, Romeo, Hamlet, Claude Melnotte, Sir Edward Mortimer, Petruchio, St. Pierre, The Stranger, Lucius Brutus*, and *Pescara*. On the 31st of August, 1857, he again appeared at the Metropolitan Theatre, and, by another brilliant series of impersonations, increased the multitude of his friendly admirers. It may be deemed worthy of note that Mr. Lawrence Barrett, — whose fidelity and professional coöperation render him good service, in these days, at his Theatre in New York — made his first appearance in that city, on the occasion of Booth's second coming to the Metropolitan, and acted *Lord Lovell*. For some time after this period the course of the tragedian lay through many wanderings in the West and South, marked by no incidents of signal import, though attended by the customary vicissitudes of a roving Thespian life. In the Summer of 1859 took place his betrothal to Mary Devlin, which was presently followed by their marriage — in the city of New York, on the 7th of July, 1860. Shortly after the wedding they set out for England.

This marriage was a very happy one, and exercised a very salutary influence upon Edwin Booth's character and professional ambition. The lady whom he espoused was one of those gentle and cheerful creatures — the incarnation of sunshine — who, by the unconscious loveliness and brightness of their lives, seem born for the express purpose of teaching happiness and hope to the duller and sadder mortals around them. She possessed the winning charm of soft and seductive personal grace. Her mind was imaginative, tasteful, keenly perceptive, sensible, and well cultivated. She was an excellent musician and a pleasing actress. Her brief existence diffused none but sweet influences, and has left none but pleasant and tender recollections. Her story, not inaptly told in this place, may be related in a few words:

Mary Devlin, the daughter of a merchant of Troy, New York, was born in that city, in 1840, and there passed her childhood's years. At a later period her education was pursued at an Institute in New York. Her tutor in music was Mrs. Seguin — whose name has been long and worthily associated with English Opera — and under this lady's care she was well grounded in the rudiments of that art. Her talent and inclination for the stage were manifested early in life; and, at length, in 1854, she made her first public appearance, at a theatre in Troy. Her best successes, at this time, were achieved in singing parts, such as *Lucy Bertram*, in "Guy Mannering," but she subsequently acquired distinction by the meritorious performance of speaking parts of a higher grade. On the 22d of June, 1858, she made her first appearance on the New York stage, acting *Juliet* to the *Romeo* of Charlotte Cushman, at Niblo's Garden. This character she also played, with marked success, at the Boston Theatre. It was a finely symmetrical personation, true and sincere in motive, and pervaded by delicious natural grace and feeling; and, by itself, it would have sufficed to win her a good professional rank. After her betrothal to Edwin Booth she retired from the stage, and she never returned to it. After her marriage, as has been stated, she accompanied her husband to England, where they remained till September, 1862. Their daughter, Edwina, was born at Fulham, near London, in the course of this period of residence abroad. On their return to America, they established their residence at Dorchester, Massachusetts. The health of Mrs. Booth had become impaired; but she was not thought to be seriously ill when her husband parted from her, to fulfill an engagement at the Winter Garden, in New York. They never met again. Her illness took a sudden and dangerous turn; she sank rapidly, and died on the 21st of February, 1863. Her grave was made at the beautiful cemetery of Mount Auburn. Few persons have been so sincerely loved or so deeply mourned. Many and affecting tributes were paid to her virtues and her memory. One of the best paintings by the artist Hennessy preserves, amid exquisitely fanciful surroundings, the image of her delicate loveliness. One of the tenderest poems of the poet Parsons (whose bright laurel will continue green when many a flourishing bay-wreath of to-day has faded and crumbled), commemorates her excellence, and utters the deep grief of many bereaved hearts:

> "She was a maiden for a man to love;
> She was a woman for a husband's life;
> One that had learned to value far above
> The name of Love, the sacred name of Wife.

> Her little life-dream, rounded so with sleep,
> Had all there is of life — except gray hairs ;
> Hope, love, trust, passion, and devotion deep,
> And that mysterious tie a Mother bears."

Reverting a single step, this chronicle touches briefly upon Edwin Booth's professional experience in England. His first engagement there was played at the Haymarket Theatre, in London, under the management of Buckstone, in September, 1861. At the instance of the manager, and contrary to his own plan and desire, he commenced as *Shylock.* The public received him kindly, but actors and critics were cold. He then acted *Sir Giles Overreach,* and closed the engagement with *Richelieu.* In the latter character — which he plays surpassingly well, and has made entirely his own — he won an instant triumph over all prejudice, and aroused a lively intellectual enthusiasm. Buckstone regretted — too late — that he had opposed the tragedian's design of beginning with this part. Booth's first performance of *Richelieu,* it may be interesting to remember, was given at Sacramento, in California, in July, 1856, and thereafter it steadily proved a source of good fortune to the actor, and of unalloyed pleasure to the public. Had he commenced with it in London — instead of commencing with a character that English critics, and the great body of play-goers, have set apart and consecrated to the memory of Edmund Kean — it seems certain that the renown and prosperity of his professional ventures abroad would have been greatly augmented. As it was, however, he made one bright mark in the British metropolis, and he came away from it in high repute.

From London he proceeded to Liverpool and Manchester; but he did not win favor in either of those cities. The great war was beginning to darken over the American Republic, and a lively dislike for "Yankees" was prevalent in those ship-building and cotton-spinning capitals. Booth seems to have received the full consequences of this sentiment. He made, therefore, no further trial of fortune in England; but, after a brief pleasure-trip to Paris, returned home, with his wife and daughter, and resumed his labors in his native land.

The old Metropolitan Theatre had now become the Winter Garden. The manager was Mr. T. B. Jackson — since deceased. The acting manager (in stage parlance), was the prince of social *farceurs,* the Momus of the banquet hall, the Democritus of journalism, William Stuart. This remarkable man — whose picturesque character, wayward life, and intellectual brilliancy, whether manifested with tongue or pen, combine to fill a very rosy ideal of the softness and brightness of Irish sentiment and humor — was destined to exercise a considerable influence upon Booth's fortunes; and their conjunction, at this time, is, therefore, a notable incident. Their first meeting had taken place several years before, at Wallack's old Theatre, on the occasion of a performance for the benefit of Mr. H. C. Jarrett, when E. L. Davenport acted *Othello*, Booth acted *Iago*, and Stuart managed the business affairs of the enterprise. They now met again, in more immediate business relations, and friendship speedily grew up between them.

Booth made his first appearance on the 29th of September, 1862, and with that date begins what may be described as the Winter Garden episode in his career. It was, perhaps, the most important period of his professional life — for it witnessed the practical utilizing of all the popularity he had previously gained, in the sure establishment of his reputation as a tragic actor of the first order. This result was brought about by means that are obviously sagacious, but difficult of practice — the conspicuous presentation of his best works in the best style. He appeared in none but good parts; he played them under none but good circumstances; and he attracted and riveted the public attention, as the central figure in a series of magnificent revivals of the standard drama. This Winter Garden episode extended from September 29th, 1862, to March 23d, 1867. During the first engagement Booth acted, in rapid succession, *Hamlet*, *Othello*, *Lucius Brutus*, *Shylock*, *Iago*, *Richelieu*, *Richard III.*, *Romeo*, *Pescara*, *Sir Edward Mortimer*, and *Don Cæsar de Bazan*. His success was unbounded. The best class of play-goers in New York attended his representations, and the discussion of them, in the newspapers, was conducted in a sympathetic and thoughtful spirit — which plainly showed that the chords of general feeling in the community had been smitten with a strong hand.

At the close of this engagement he set off, under cheerful auspices, on a professional tour of the large cities of the Union. On the 9th of February, 1863, he returned to the Winter Garden, and again appeared as *Hamlet;* but this time he was "under a cloud" — ill in mind and body, unnerved and depressed by a gloomy presentiment of impending evil. The engagement, prematurely broken, lasted only till the 20th of February, and comprised only eleven performances. On its last night the actor was summoned to the bed-side of his dying wife. He went at once — but he reached home only to find its light extinguished, its music hushed, and its fair spirit departed. Thus once more a bitter bereavement laid upon his life the heavy burden of affliction and sorrow.

Booth now relinquished his Dorchester residence, purchased a house in New York, abandoned his profession, and went into retirement, with his mother — contemplating a long seclusion from public life. As the year wore on, however, he began to feel the necessity of occupation. The dreams and plans of an earlier time came back upon his mind; the wish to "shine in use" rather than to "rust unburnished" woke again, and asserted its former power; and at length he determined to improve opportunities which then presented themselves of embarking with his brother-in-law, Mr. John S. Clarke, the celebrated comedian, in two theatrical enterprises of magnitude and importance. One of these was the purchase of the Walnut Street Theatre, in Philadelphia; the other was the hiring of the Winter Garden Theatre, in New York. Both were speedily undertaken; and it is needless to say that they at once opened a field for the energetic exercise of great and various ability. In the management of the Philadelphia house, Booth and Clarke were associated from the Summer of 1863 till March, 1870, when the latter purchased his partner's interest. In the management of the Winter Garden they associated with themselves Mr. William Stuart — to whom allusion has been made — and by this triumvirate the theatre was conducted during the greater part of the rest of its existence. The history of this theatre in detail might prove an interesting narrative to theatrical readers, but it would not be quite appropriate here — the purpose of this sketch being to condense into a clear and rapid statement the chief events in Booth's individual experience as an actor, rather than to dwell at length upon particular phases of his labor, or matters incidental to his business undertakings. In the direct course of personal record, then, it is next to be noted that the first season of the Winter Garden, under its new management, began on the 21st of September, 1863, when Booth reappeared as *Hamlet*. He was welcomed by the public with ardent cordiality, and he played a remarkably prosperous engagement — extending to the 17th of October. Towards its close he acted, for the first time, *Ruy Blas*. Wanderings, in the usual track, followed this period of metropolitan effort; but by the ensuing Spring these had ended, and on the 28th of March, 1864, he once more claimed the attention of the New York public, appearing at Niblo's Garden, and winning a golden triumph — one of the brightest of his life — as *Bertuccio*, in "The Fool's Revenge." This play is a three-act version, made by Mr. Tom Taylor, of Victor Hugo's "Le Roi S'Amuse." In it an outraged husband and father, blindly pursuing a scheme of vengeance upon his wronger, is made to assist a libertine in the forcible abduction of his own daughter. This father is the Fool, and this is his Revenge. He subsequently discovers his mistake, and when he does so he suffers a revulsion of feeling and a strong shock of agony to which no words can afford adequate expression. The character makes a deep draught upon imagination and sensibility. Booth's personation of it was wonderfully vivid and magnetic. Fierce vitality, bitter, sardonic humor, and mad vindictiveness made the embodiment absolutely fiendish — a horrible incarnation of gleeful wickedness and insane fury. But, through all this there ran a golden vein of pathos. At one time the actor seemed like Alecto raving in the infernal pit. This was when, under the night sky and in the lonely street, *Bertuccio* calls down upon his enemy the tortures which have so long burned and raged in his own bosom. At another time he was as pitiable as *Lear* himself, in the climax of his awful agony. This was in a scene outside the door of the banquet hall, when the Fool pleads for admittance, to rescue his daughter. The simulation of glee, through which the father's frantic grief and terror broke, at last, in wild and lamentable cries of anguish, was one of the finest things ever done by an actor, and one of the most thrilling expositions that Booth ever afforded of the power of his genius and the magic of his art. This performance, painful and terrible though it was, won him a great deal of admiration, and gave to students of his acting some entirely new views of the originality and versatility of his mind.

He was also seen, during this engagement at Niblo's, as *Raphael*, in "The Marble Heart," which he then played for the first time in New York. This was on the 18th of April, 1864. On the 16th he had acted *Sir Edward Mortimer* and *Petruchio*, for the benefit of the American Sanitary Fair. The engagement terminated on the 22d, and he at once resumed his labors at the Winter Garden.

Shakspeare's birthday, the 23d, was celebrated by the production of "Romeo and Juliet," for the benefit of the Fund for erecting a monument to the Poet in the Central Park — Mr. Hackett playing *Falstaff*, at Niblo's Garden, on the same night, in aid of the same cause. Booth continued to act at the Winter Garden till the 14th of May, appearing as *Hamlet, Othello, Richelieu*, and *Richard III*. A Summer of preparation succeeded, with a view to the first of those dramatic pageants by which he has done so much to delight and instruct the community, to dignify the American stage, and to gild his own name with respect and honor. "Hamlet" was brought out on the 21st of November, 1864, and it kept the stage till the 24th of March, 1865 — greeted, at the outset, with ardent public enthusiasm, and sustained till the end by a sincere — though, of course, gradually lessening — public interest. This was the period that saw accomplished for "Hamlet" the celebrated run of one hundred nights. It was a superb revival. The scenery, devised with scholarship and taste, and executed at large expense, presented a series of veritable gems of illusion. The views of the churchyard by moonlight and the battlements of the castle of Elsinore were, in particular, exceedingly beautiful. A cold wind of death seemed to shrill around the dusky, sombre towers, as the dread ghost came floating in before the stricken gaze of the terrified midnight watchers. Booth played *Hamlet* with a lofty purity and abstraction of spirit, and a fineness of method, that he had never before attained. It was recognized as his greatest achievement in art, and such it remains to the present day. Many writers recorded its merits and celebrated its excellence — discussing it with thoughtful care and profound sympathy. Seldom has the work of an actor concentrated upon itself, in an equal degree, the attention of judicious intellect and the generous enthusiasm of the popular heart. Eloquent illustration of the interest it excited might readily be gleaned from the numerous commemorative articles of the time. One of these, written by George William Curtis, in *Harper's Magazine* for April, 1865, contains passages especially worthy of reproduction here, because they pay a just tribute, from an authoritative source, and in graceful and fitting terms, to a noble and beautiful work of art:

" A really fine actor is as uncommon as a really great dramatic poet. Yet what Garrick was in *Richard III.*, or Edmund Kean in *Shylock*, we are sure Edwin Booth is in *Hamlet*. . The scenery was thoughtfully studied and the effect was entirely harmonious. . . . . . Booth looks the ideal *Hamlet*. For the *Hamlet* of our imaginations, which is the *Hamlet* of Shakspeare, is not the ' scant of breath ' gentleman whom the severer critics insist that he should be. He is a sad, slight Prince. . . Booth is altogether princely. His costume is still the solemn suit of sables, varied according to his fancy of greater fitness, and his small, lithe form, with the mobility and intellectual sadness of his face, and his large melancholy eyes, satisfy the most fastidious imagination that this is *Hamlet* as he lived in Shakspeare's world. His playing throughout has an exquisite tone, like an old picture. The charm of the finest portraits, of Raphael's Julius or Leo, of Titian's Francis I., or Ippolito di Medici, of Vandyck's Charles I., is not the drawing nor even the coloring, so much as the nameless, subtle harmony which is called tone. So in Booth's *Hamlet* it is not any particular scene, or passage, or look, or movement that conveys the impression ; it is the consistency of every part with every other, the pervasive sense of the mind of a true gentleman sadly strained and jarred. Through the whole play the mind is borne on in mournful reverie. It is not so much what he says or does that we observe ; for under all, beneath every scene and word and act, we hear what is not audible, the melancholy music of the sweet bells jangled, out of tune, and harsh. This gives a curious reality to the whole. Booth's conception of *Hamlet* is that of a morbid mind, conscious of its power to master the mystery

of life, which in its details, baffles and overwhelms him. There is, therefore, a
serene consciousness of superiority in his behavior, even in the most perplexed
moments. In the chamber scene with his mother, when the ghost passes and
Hamlet falls for a moment prostrate with emotion at his disappearance, the Queen
insinuates that he is mad. There is a kind of calm, pitying disdain, mingled with
the sense that her feeling is natural, with which *Hamlet* steps toward her, his
finger on his pulse. The tragedy in *Hamlet* is not only the vital curiosity about
existence, the mastering love of life which almost subdues his soul with fear and
doubt, and keeps it tense with eager questioning; but it is the conviction of a
mind morbid with this continual strain that it is a most sacred duty to end
another life, to plunge a guilty soul into the abyss of doubt, and that soul the one
dearest to his mother. This explains the fascination which the idea of his uncle's
death always exercises upon his mind, and also his inability to do more than
dream and doubt over the action. It is this complication which produces one of
Booth's finest scenes. In the interview with his mother he stabs *Polonius* through
the arras. For an instant the possibility of what he has done sweeps over his
mind. Always the victim of complex emotions, the instinctive satisfaction of
knowing the act done is mingled with the old familiar horror of the doom to
which he may have consigned his uncle. With sword uplifted, and a vague terror
both of hope and fear in his face and tone, *Hamlet* does not slide rapidly back
and hurriedly exclaim, 'Is it the king?' but tottering with emotion he asks slowly,
in an appalling staccato, 'Is — it — the — king?' The cumulative sadness
of the play was never so palpable as in Booth's acting. It is a spell from which
you cannot escape."

Booth's *Hamlet*, withdrawn from the Winter Garden stage on the 24th of
March, 1865, was immediately transferred to that of the Boston Theatre, at which
house the tragedian was acting when — a little later, on the 14th of April — a sudden
and fearful calamity overwhelmed and well-nigh ruined him. All the world knows
what it was. The whole people of America and the heart of all Christendom
suffered in it a terrible shock and a bitter bereavement. Consternation, grief and
rage swept over the land. The excitement of that baleful hour — still vivid in
public remembrance — was wild and indiscriminate; and, very naturally, the relatives
of the wretched maniac, who took the life of President Lincoln, incurred, and
suffered under, the odium of unjust suspicion and popular resentment. The knowledge that a brother's hand was thus steeped in guilt and ignominy was — it
may well be conceived — a heavy weight of woe to Edwin Booth. Immediate
and superficial troubles, incident to the horrid experience, could be endured and

surmounted; but the sense of the crime itself, as done, in all its awful wicked-ness and madness, by one of his own birth and blood, imposed upon his sensitive, conscientious, proud, and reticent nature an acute and immedicable anguish. For a time his hard-earned reputation, the honor of his name, and the station and repute of his family seemed utterly destroyed. Life, in the present, was a blank; and beyond the present a waste of misery stretched into the future. He at once left the stage and buried himself in obscurity: and from that retirement he would never have emerged, but for the stern necessity of meeting pecuniary obligations, incurred long before, and only to be met through his active resump-tion of professional industry. The softening and cheering influence of public sympathy — which presently began to set toward him in a strong tide of interest — gave, it is true, a certain persuasiveness to this voice of duty, and rendered obedience to its mandate a far more facile and agreeable task than it could otherwise have been. Had there not existed, however, an imperative necessity that Edwin Booth should return to the stage, he would never have acted again. He reappeared on the 3rd of January, 1866, at the Winter Garden Theatre, in the character of *Hamlet*. An immense throng of persons gave him welcome — and it was such a welcome as might well have lightened the saddest heart and the most anxious mind. Nine cheers hailed the melancholy Dane upon his first entrance. The spectators rose, and waved their hats and handkerchiefs. Bouquets fell in a shower upon the stage. There was a tempest of applause: and the affectionate sympathy which beamed in every face and trembled in every voice gave assurance, deep and strong, that the generous public had no idea of heaping upon an innocent man the burden and blight of a guilty brother's crime. At the hands of the Press — which has, all along, bestowed a great friendship upon Edwin Booth — he received the same cordial treatment. Nor was the welcome less kind, in communities out of New York. Wherever he appeared, after this momentous return to the stage, he found a free-hearted greeting and respectful sympathy; and so, little by little, he got back into the old way of work, and his professional career resumed its flow in the old channel.

The second of those sumptuous revivals of the legitimate drama with which, in the minds of the play-going public, the name of Edwin Booth is inseparably associated, was made after his return to the stage, in 1866. Preparations for this had been commenced prior to the great disaster which led to his retirement; and, under the careful and tireless conduct of Mr. Stuart, these, when resumed, were speedily completed. The play was "Richelieu," and this was brought

forward at the Winter Garden on the 1st of February. The scenery, painted
by Witham, Van Hanleim, and Hilliard, made up a pageant of extraordinary
splendor. One picture, in particular, was a gem of imaginative composition.
It represented an apartment in the Cardinal's Palace at Ruell. The perspective
was composed of dim arches. A flood of cold, pale moonlight streamed
in through a lofty gothic window, and faintly illumined the rich, quaint, sombre
furniture. On the carved table stood a candelabrum, with flaring lights. This
is the scene in which the withered but fiery ecclesiastic — awaiting the arrival
of *Francois*, with the packet that will place the conspirators within his grip, pores
upon a book and reads the sage counsel of the sober moralist. . Booth's *Richelieu* —
always a majestic presence, instinct with electric life — showed with singular dis-
tinctness and beauty, amid these poetic accessories. There were other rich
embellishments: but these mentioned may suffice to indicate the care and taste
with which the whole work was accomplished. In respect to magnificence and
elaboration, the effect of this revival has been surpassed, in the more recent production of " Richelieu," at Booth's Theatre (1871); but its plan, then fully matured
and fairly tried, has ever since been followed as a guide and model. It was on
the occasion of this presentment of " Richelieu," by the way, that the expedient
was first adopted of putting the Court of Louis XIII. into mourning, in view of
the supposed death of the Cardinal. Booth's personation of *Richelieu* has, by
many acute critics, been accounted his best work of art. Caldwell, of New
Orleans, the veteran manager — whose great experience and sagacity made him a
very competent judge — singled out this performance, at an early period in the
actor's career, as the best, and certain to become the most popular; and he
advised the tragedian always to give it when newly appearing in any place. The
character is one that assimilates, at many points, with Edwin Booth's temperament
and one that is marvelously well adapted to catch the sympathies of mankind.
Appearing as the soldier-priest, the tragedian has never failed to win the popular
heart. No piece of acting is better known in this generation, and — except it
be Jefferson's matchless performance of *Rip Van Winkle* — no piece of acting is
more admired. To offer any new observation on a topic so exceedingly familiar
would be very difficult. Perhaps the present writer may best serve the purpose
of the immediate occasion by reproducing some remarks of his own, originally
published elsewhere (New York *Tribune*, January 12th, 1871), which duly com-
memorate this fine achievement:

   " ' Richelieu ' stands in the front rank of romantic plays. It embodies a story
of perspicuous simplicity, and yet of enthralling interest. It presents clearly

defined characters, in natural relations to one another. It is inspired by a steady dramatic movement that increases in speed and rises in force, attaining an electrical climax and a beautiful culmination. It is adequately provided — without being overwhelmed — with situations that excite the mind and touch the heart. Its spirit is sympathetic with virtue and gentleness, and thereby it captivates the general instincts of human nature. Above all, it is imaginative. It idealizes reality, and does not pretend to present character and experience in the humdrum garb of prosy fact. Considered as an ideal creation, it is a drama without a serious defect. Its sole important blemish is a blemish of literary art. There is some tinsel in the lines — something of the paste-diamond element, that seems to be a portion of its author's mind. Little faults, however, dwindle out of sight in the presence of great merits. 'Richelieu' is a work that constantly affords pleasure, by celebrating the victory of goodness over evil, under deeply interesting and vividly picturesque conditions of circumstance; and to have written a drama that thus accomplishes the distinct result of making its spectators happier and better is really to have deserved the gratitude of mankind. No considerate critic, therefore, will dwell upon a blemish so slight as an occasional tawdry line in a work so truly powerful and brilliant. Bulwer-Lytton is a benefactor to all who love and enjoy the stage, and as such he merits honor and gratitude.

"Booth's *Richelieu* is one of the most powerful, symmetrical, and picturesque works of dramatic art with which the stage is adorned. It may not reproduce the Cardinal of history. That result was not essential. It certainly does embody the Cardinal of the drama. Grave doubts may well be entertained whether *Richelieu* was the noble spirit in actual life that he is in this rosy fiction. No doubt whatever can be entertained that the poet has depicted him as just, wise, kind, gentle, tolerant of weakness, sympathetic with goodness, sensitive to every sweet and poetic influence, and only inimical to tyranny and wrong. The lower side of his nature is its craft; but it is the craft of a philosopher and not of a sneak. If he uses indirection, it is such indirection as a deep knowledge of human nature and affairs has taught him to be essential in the conduct of his life and the government of mankind. He never resorts to the skin of the fox till he has first exhausted the skin of the lion. In this drama he is shown to be engaged upon comparatively small matters — the protection of a pair of lovers and the defeat of a political intrigue; but he is steadily presented as a man of the most potent intellect, and the purest and liveliest sensibility. In other words, he is seen to have a background of strong character, a stately and picturesque individuality, in despite of his little vanities and of the littleness of the designs amid which he moves. The magnetic charm of the character doubtless grows out of precisely this relation. It is the embodiment of virtuous power shown in its grandest phase and function, as the protector of innocent weakness. Booth has grasped this idea and made it the vital spirit of his personation. That he looks the character is a matter of course. His weird, thoughtful, spiritual face and his slender, priest-like figure — made up with the concomitants of age and clothed in the requisite and accurate ecclesiastical garments — combine in a perfect present-ment of the fiery soul in the aged and puny body. The physical realization could not be improved. And it has this great merit — that it has grown out of a combination of intuitions, and crystallized upon a distinct ideal. Form, we need not say, is a trivial matter unless it be eloquent with spirit. That eloquence pervades and illuminates Booth's *Richelieu.* Seeing the aged priest and hearing his voice, one instinctively feels, without pausing to reflect upon it, that this is a grand and noble old man, in whom the affections live an immortal life, who will be true as steel to all that is good and pure, who wears with authentic right the imperial garb of power, and who must as inevitably conquer as the sun must rise. To take this identity, to preserve it, to show many phases of the same nature, and yet retain the same poetic individuality, is greatly to succeed in the art of acting; and that is what Booth accomplishes in his performance of *Richelieu.*"

Affairs at the Winter Garden went on, in the customary hum-drum routine of all theatrical life, for another year. Most of the time Booth was absent, on professional expeditions in divers parts of the country. With the first days of 1867, however, came the maturity of another professional enterprise, in which he and his partners had labored with assiduous zeal, and the results of which were seen in the sumptuous presentation of "The Merchant of Venice," made at the Winter Garden, on the 28th of January. This beautiful drama was brought forward in a singularly beautiful dress. Hilliard and Witham painted the scenes — from sketches made by the lamented Leutze. The chief pictures showed the Rialto, the Church of San Giovanni, the Place of St. Mark, a hall in Portia's house, and the Venetian Senate Chamber. Upon the walls of the latter — as a fact indicative of the thorough care with which this pageantry was devised — it may be noted that there hung several excellent copies of paintings by Tintoretto. An unusual refinement of taste was expended on the garden scene, which reflected, in a remarkable way, the sweet sentiment and delicious langour that charac-terize a Summer landscape. Booth acted *Shylock.* The character is an embodied protest against cruel wrongs inflicted by a powerful oppressor upon an outlawed nation. To the Jew, as a usurer and a hater, it would be impossible to render more adequate justice than was done in Booth's performance; but to the Jew, as an intellectual and majestic representative of the Mosaic law, and as an outraged and heart-broken parent, he did not impart all the requisite stateliness nor all the indispensable wildness and pathos of conflicting anguish and suppressed passion. Such, at any rate, was the impression of the present writer. Other opinions accepted the performance as thoroughly Shakspearean; and, certainly it was full of fiery life. An eloquent review of it, written at the time by Mr. William Stuart, was one of the best tributes it evoked from the Press; and from this a brief descriptive extract may here properly find a place:

"Booth possesses for this, as for so many other characters, physical advantages which alone carry a talismanic charm. As he enters on the stage it needs but a glance to see that not the gabardine alone proclaims the Jew nor the Hebrew cap marks the nation. Around the ancient figure, clad by Booth in Eastern garb, of most picturesque correctness, there hangs a certain halo of grace which is eminently characteristic. In the downcast look there is an air of selfish isolation. In the large, dark eyes there burns the fierce light of centuries of wrong. In all the externals are those contrasts of color in which Rembrandt, in his picture of the Jew, delights to revel. Then in the acting, Booth imparts to the character its primitive Shakspearean dignity. He does not rail at the Christian merchant, and then cajole him — rendering him, as so many do, an arrant idiot; but he pleasantly beguiles him into the merry bond, showing only by a momentary fiendish glance the malignant purpose which lurks beneath. This toning down at the commencement has the effect, too, of bringing out in stronger contrast the splendid burst of passion in the third act, in which the rapid transitions from the wildest expression of joy to the most abject misery were portrayed by Booth, now with a fire and vigor, and again with a depth of pathos, which thrilled the audience and completely swept the house. His bearing in the trial scene, too, was as defined and finished as a perfect piece of statuary. It was impossible to look on that face and form, so full of sullen, dark, determined malignity, and, at the same time, of patriarchal grandeur, without feeling that there stood, indeed, the Jew whom Shakspeare imagined. Among the many beauties with which the trial-scene was strewn may be mentioned Booth's restless impatience at the delay of justice, for *Solanio;* the keen and wolfish glare he fastens and keeps fixed upon his expected victim; the cold shudder of horror with which he catches the first word about his becoming Christian; and the effort he makes to get up one bold look at the jeering *Gratiano,* — after which, from the force of abject habit, and defeat, he drops his lids, and staggers out, in silent communing with his broken and baffled spirit. These were a few exquisite touches scattered among the more massive strokes of art. Indeed, from the first, Booth gathered, · with the spell of genius, the interest of the audience into his grasp, and held it to the close ; and his *Shylock* may well claim a place alongside of *Hamlet* and *Richelieu* in that gallery of art he is creating, to adorn and enrich the drama."

It was during this engagement — on the night of January 22d, 1867 — that Booth received the Hamlet Medal. This was an offering, indicative of appreciation and respect, from many of the chief citizens of New York, students of Shakspeare, and friends of the stage. The presentation took place publicly, at the close of the performance of " Hamlet," and in the presence of a great concourse of the people. The stage was set to represent a drawing-room, arriving in which the Presentation Committee met the actor, in the dress of *Hamlet* — the united bands of the principal theatres in New York, playing, meanwhile, the Danish National Hymn. Amongst the numerous gentlemen who appeared on the stage were Admiral Farragut; Admiral Palmer; Major General Robert Anderson; John T. Hoffman, Governor of New York; George Bancroft, the Historian; Charles A. Dana; Judge C. P. Daly; Albert Bierstadt, and Jervis McEntee, artists; and Messrs. Richard O'Gorman, and William Fullerton, members of the New York Bar. The latter gentleman, giving earnest and happy expression to the general esteem in which the tragedian is cherished, spoke the following graceful and appropriate words :

" Mr. Booth: You have deservedly won a position in your profession which few men have ever attained. The representation of one of Shakspeare's plays for one hundred consecutive nights to overflowing and delighted audiences is a triumph unrecorded in the annals of the stage until you accomplished it, and is well worthy of commemoration. But it is not alone your success as an actor which has attracted public attention and called forth this demonstration. You have won alike the applause and respect of your fellow men ; and a numerous body of your friends and admirers, through their Committee, now here present, desire to present you with some evidence of their appreciation of your genius as an actor, and their respect for you as a man, more substantial and enduring than the fleeting though hearty plaudits nightly heard within these walls. To that end they have instructed me to present you with this medal. Intrinsically it is of little worth ; but as a token of the regard of your fellow-citizens it possesses a significance far more valuable than the gold of which it is composed or the artistic skill which has beautified it. It was thought proper that this presentation should take place on the occasion of the play of "Hamlet," with which your name will ever be associated, and on the very spot of your greatest professional achievements — thereby affording your numerous friends an opportunity of witnessing it. But the choice of time and place for this ceremony has another and a deeper meaning. It intends a recognition of your life-long efforts to raise the moral standard of the drama, and to encourage you in your future endeavors to accomplish that result. In conclusion, I beg you to accept this gift; and, at the same time, allow me to express the universal wish that you may live to win new triumphs in a profession which your virtues have elevated and your talents adorned."

The Medal is made of gold, is oval in form, and is surrounded by a golden serpent. In the centre is Booth's head, as *Hamlet.* At the top is the Danish crown, from which hang two wreaths, on either side, of laurel and myrtle. The pin, from which the Medal depends, has, in the centre, a head of Shakspeare, with heads emblematic of comedy and tragedy on each side. The motto is, *Palmam qui meruit ferat.* The inscription reads as follows:

To

EDWIN BOOTH:

*In commemoration of the unprecedented run of "Hamlet," as enacted by him
in New York City for one hundred nights.*

The hour of doom for the Winter Garden Theatre was now close at hand. By way of giving zest and freshness to the close of his engagements, it had, all along, been Booth's custom to dedicate the final week in each of them to that variety which the public always approves. The custom was followed now, as it had been before. The last week of this engagement in 1867 — which was also the last in the record of the theatre — began on the 18th of March. Booth played, on four successive nights, *Pescara, Hamlet, Othello,* and *Sir Giles.* On the fifth he appeared as *Lucius Brutus.* This was the night of the 22d of March. Fire is used in one scene of Payne's tragedy, and this is thought to have been the germ of the conflagration that followed. Towards morning, on the 23rd, flames burst forth, underneath the stage, and thence spread so swiftly, and raged with so much fury, that all efforts to save the property were baffled, and persons in the building had some difficulty in saving themselves. Mr. Stuart, who occupied apartments in the theatre —memorable as the haunt of genial spirits and the scene of social and intellectual festivity — narrowly escaped a dreadful death. In a few hours the theatre was a ruin. With it perished all the sumptuous scenery that had been provided for "Hamlet," "Richelieu," and "The Merchant of Venice;" the whole of Booth's personal wardrobe, including several articles of stage-dress that had been worn by his father; a large and rich collection of stage dresses appertaining to the theatre; a great mass of theatrical furniture; valuable clothes and jewels owned by members of the dramatic company; a quantity of costly armor; a considerable library, inclusive of several important manuscripts; and one of the most interesting galleries of theatrical portraits that have been made in this country. Betterton, Garrick, Foote, Cooke, Kean, Kemble, Young, Siddons, O'Neil, Fairbrother, the elder Mathews, the elder Booth, and Macready — with many more of ancient and honorable renown — looked down from the walls of the guest-room, and presented the storied Past to the homage of the ' admiring Present. These losses, very serious to Booth's business-manager and sole remaining partner, Mr. Stuart (for Clarke, with singular good fortune, had sold his interest in the theatre to Booth, just prior to the disaster), fell with especial force upon the tragedian himself, striking his gained success out of his grasp, setting him back on the current of enterprise, and making triumphs, that before had been close at hand, conditional now on years of added toil. That he possessed the public sympathy, however, was, in some sense, comfortable encouragement, for it implied that, in any new project he might attempt, he could confidently count on the public support. Indications of that sympathy were abundant and emphatic. It was seen in prosperous benefit performances, for sufferers by the fire. It was seen in the assurances of aid, toward erecting a new theatre, from private friends. It was notably seen in the tone of the Press. The Winter Garden — largely by reason of Mr. Stuart's cheerfulness, Celtic humor, and intellectual magnetism — had become the especial favorite of journalists; and by these, accordingly, its loss was sincerely mourned. From one contemporary tribute, typical of many, a brief extract, commemorative of the scene of famous art triumphs and much genuine happiness, may here be cited:

"The loss of the Winter Garden is a public no less than a private, calamity. The extent of that calamity will not be at once realized. Sorrow that is recent, is, for that very reason, indefinite. But as days go by, the void that has been left in the dramatic world will become more and more conspicuous, and memory will more and more define, color, linger upon, and grieve over this sudden and sharp bereavement. It is no common chance that has destroyed, not alone the richest scenic treasures ever collected in this country, but a place that garnered up bright recollections of a memorable past, and fair promises and high hopes of the future of the drama. We cannot dismiss the burning of the Winter Garden as a commonplace incident in that long chapter of haps and mishaps which comprises the news of the day. To tell the story of the conflagration is but partially to fulfill the duty of the moment. That duty also prescribes reflection upon the associations that made the place so gracious, and upon the promise that slumbers in its ashes. A record that extends over but little more than twelve years is not, of course, impressive on the score of antiquity. But the record of this theatre, brief though it be, is brilliant. Here sounded the heavenly voice of Jenny Lind. Here glided the weird, terrible, ineffably beauteous form of Rachel. Here the quaint visage and the mellow tones of Burton gladdened all hearts to laughter or saddened them to tears. Here Agnes Robertson played, in the prime of her touching and winning sweetness. Poor old Blake acted here — next to Burton the most humorous man of his generation. Here the genius of Jefferson cast its spell over many a heart. Here Brougham has won his best triumphs in the full celebrity of his sparkling talent. Miss Bateman began here that dramatic career which has been a continuous triumph. The piquant and dazzling Cubas danced here, and taught us the poetry of sunny Spain. On this stage the rare talent and the polished skill of Clarke gained the whole-hearted recognition of critical and popular applause. Here too the public heart was captured by the extraordinary magnetism of Matilda Heron, in her memorable personation of *Camille*. From this theatre, after a series of most intellectual and powerful performances, was uttered the farewell word of Charlotte Cushman. Here, finally — for the list must somewhere cease — Edwin Booth accomplished what no one had ever accomplished before, the successful representation, for a hundred nights, of the tragedy of 'Hamlet.' Such are some of the achievements — now traditions — that have given to the Winter Garden the lustre of renown. It is natural that such a theatre should have been affectionately prized, and that its loss should be deeply deplored. The friends of the drama, those who have wished it well, watched over it, labored for its support, and claimed for it a high place among the educating influences of the age, have ever found, and have been proud and happy to find, that the management of the Winter Garden has been conducted in a cultured and honorable spirit. We speak of triumphs that are yet recent when we refer to the magnificent production here of the plays of 'Hamlet,' 'Richelieu,' and 'The Merchant of Venice.' These enterprises were not alone the exponents of a wise and noble ambition ; they were also the guarantees of still more splendid efforts in the future. It is pleasant now to say, and to say it on behalf of all votaries of the drama, and to say it to Mr. Booth and Mr. Stuart in their time of sore distress, that they have wrought greatly in a great work; that they have set a splendid example of reverence for, and devotion to, the drama; and that no misfortune can ever cloud their triumph. The fact that a high, broad, and honest devotion to a noble art has animated and controlled their past career, is the promise that sleeps in the ashes of the Winter Garden. Human activity so inspired can never be defeated. A new theatre must arise out of the ruins of the old one. The losses that have been suffered must all be repaired. The successes of the past must be repeated and augmented in the future."

These words — quoted, not inaptly it is hoped, from a contemporary article by the writer of this sketch.— embodied a prophetic promise that has been amply and brilliantly fulfilled. The Winter Garden was destroyed on the 23d of March, 1867. The corner-stone of Booth's Theatre was laid on the 8th of April, 1868 — and the first performance in the new house took place on the 3rd of February, 1869. This contrast of facts very clearly implies that no grass was permitted to grow on the path of this worthy enterprise. The project for the new theatre was, indeed, suggested to Booth within a very brief period after the loss of the old one. It originated with Mr. Richard A. Robertson — acting upon whose proposition Booth entered into a partnership with him, for the establishment of the house that is now famous as BOOTH'S THEATRE. Immediate steps were taken toward the fulfillment of their design. During the Spring of 1867, Mr. J. H. Magonigle, their business representative — now the manager of the theatre — inspected various eligible building-sites, and ultimately selected and purchased the lot on the south-east corner of Twenty-Third Street and Sixth Avenue, in the city of New York. The work of establishing the New Theatre was commenced on the 1st of July, in the same year. A number of houses standing upon the land had first to be removed; and, when this had been done, the solid stone ledge beneath them had to be blasted out. But the labor was prosecuted with great energy and despatch, so that by the 8th of April, 1868, the corner-stone of the new theatre could be laid. It was a cold and blustering day, and only a few persons were present to witness the ceremony. Mr. James H. Hackett — to mention whom is to think of the best living representative of *Falstaff*, and one of the most loving and erudite students of Shakspeare — performed the official ceremony and pronounced an address. Judge C. P. Daly, the well-known Shakspearean scholar, spoke also, and — tempering grave thoughts with refined pleasantry — said that the drama was cradled in a booth, and that by a Booth it would be perpetuated. Then, with the usual Masonic observances, the stone was settled into its place. In the box placed beneath it were deposited these articles:

A narrative of the causes which led to the building of the theatre, engrossed on parchment. A "Tercentenary Badge," embossed on silk : this ornament was worn by the devotees of Shakspeare, in commemoration of the three-hundredth anniversary of his birthday : It is inscribed with a portrait of the poet, a view of his birth-place, and a view of the church that contains his grave. A photograph of a bust of Shakspeare, with eleven views of Stratford-on-Avon. A copy of the Life of Junius Brutus Booth, written by his daughter, Mrs. Asia Booth Clarke. Two photographs of the elder Booth, from the excellent bust by Gould. A miniature plaster cast of the head of Edwin Booth. Two photographs of Edwin Booth. A copy of Shakspeare's "Hamlet," as produced by Edwin Booth and William Stuart, at the Winter Garden Theatre, in 1864, when the tragedy was represented for one hundred consecutive nights. A copy of Lord Lytton's "Richelieu," as revived and produced at the same theatre. Two photographs of J. H. Hackett. Two circulars, contributed by Mr. Hackett, in relation to the Central Park Monument, commenced on the three-hundredth anniversary of the Birth of Shakspeare. A copy of an oration in defence of the Stage, by W. Correll. Documents relating to the Hamlet Medal Presentation to Edwin Booth. Pamphlets on scientific subjects. A collection of play-bills of the present day. A number of ancient and modern coins. A file of the leading daily journals of New York City. A complete copy of Shakspeare's Works.

Booth's theatre is made of granite — and is made to last. The front of the structure, on Twenty-Third Street, is 184 feet in length — the theatre front measuring 150 feet. The other 34 feet is the width of a wing of the main building, which abuts upon its west end, and has a frontage of 76 feet on the Sixth Avenue. The lower part of this wing is occupied by stores, while the upper part contains offices, studios, and miscellaneous rooms. The theatre is 100 feet deep, from north to south ; and 120 feet in height. The main entrance opens from Twenty-Third Street, but there is another large entrance opening from the Sixth Avenue. At the east end of the front is a great door to the stage, corresponding in size and style with the main entrance to the auditorium. Between these are three smaller doors, which are used as means of exit. Three large panels surmount these doors, which are to contain sculptured bas-reliefs. All the doors are arched. Higher up, and placed equi-distant along the front of the theatre, are three large alcoves, framed in Ionic pillars, which are to contain statues, in white marble. An effigy of Shakspeare will stand in the central arch, and emblematic figures of tragedy and comedy will occupy the others. There are four large and handsome windows on a line with these alcoves. Above runs a beautiful cornice, and above this the side slopes inward to meet the roof, which is surmounted by three short towers. In the front of each tower there is an oval window, surrounded by elaborate carvings. A flag-staff rises from the centre of the flat roof. Around the summit of each tower runs an ornamental trellis-work of iron; and, artfully placed on the lightning-rods which trail over towers and roof, are gilded stars and crescents. Entering at the principal door, the visitor finds himself in a commodious vestibule paved with Italian marble tiling, and lined with Italian marble cement — the ceiling being frescoed. This vestibule extends in a semi-circle along the rear of the auditorium, to which entrance is afforded by three arched doors. The lower floor of the theatre comprises the divisions of parquette and orchestra. A spacious stone staircase, at the south end of the vestibule, leads to the balcony. Midway on this staircase is Thomas E. Gould's marble bust of the elder Booth. Above the balcony is a second gallery, and above that is the amphitheatre, which is reached by a stone staircase from the vestibule within the Sixth Avenue entrance. There are three proscenium boxes on each side of the stage, and the house affords comfortable seats for 1,700 persons, besides standing room for at least 300 more. In shape, the auditorium follows the old horse-shoe model — but this has been so skillfully modified as to result in a shape of unusual and delightful symmetry. From every part of the theatre the stage can be distinctly seen. Bright frescoes shine forth on the ceilings. A vast chandelier depends from the centre of the roof. All the gas-jets in the building are ignited by electricity. The ornamentation of the proscenium is simple and beautiful. Marble pillars, adorned with statuesque figures, arise on either side of the boxes. In the centre of the arch above, a massive statue of Shakspeare is placed — the work of Signor Turini, an Italian artist. It represents the poet meditating, and in act to write. Other statues and emblematic devices surround this figure and complete the decoration of the arch. There is a neatly designed pit for the musical band, sunk below the front of the stage, and below the level of the main floor, so that the performers do not obstruct the view of the stage from the auditorium. Sitting in the amphitheatre, the spectator faces the wall above the proscenium arch, whereon are portrait busts — excellent likenesses — of Garrick, Talma, Edmund Kean, George Frederick Cooke, and Betterton. These are in white ovals, which are relieved against a background of rich color. Overhead, in an ascending perspective, is an elaborate painting, emblematic of the triumph of the Muse. From the centre of this depends the chandelier. On the walls, immediately beneath the ceiling, are various emblematic figures and devices. One panel represents Venus, in her chariot. Another depicts the march of Cupid. On the right hand are figures of *Lear* and *Hamlet*. On the left are figures of *Othello* and *Macbeth*. Above the proscenium arch, and under the statue of Shakspeare, is painted that coat-of-arms which John Shakspeare got from the King-at-Arms, Robert Cook. The stage is equally excellent with the rest of the house. The distance from the footlights to the rear wall is 55 feet, and the stage is 76 feet wide. Beneath it is a pit 32 feet deep, that was blasted out of the solid rock. This useful chasm is neatly paved with brick. An entire scene can be sunk into it, out of sight. On the stage, as in every other part of the theatre, double floors are laid, and the flooring of the stage is secured entirely by screws — not a single nail being anywhere driven. In each of the rear corners of the stage is a spiral staircase, which leads to the fly-galleries, high up beneath the roof. These galleries are four in number, two upon each side. Between them, up aloft, depends the complex machinery requisite for lifting and lowering the scenes. There are no obstructions upon the stage, no dressing-rooms there, none of those dirty and mysterious burrows which make many other stages look like slices out of chaos. Ample space, on the contrary, is afforded, every particle of which ripe skill has utilized, and over which the great instinct of order imperiously presides. At the south side of the stage is the scene-room, thoroughly stocked with scenery. Above this, is the paint-room, 57 feet by 16 feet, in which a flat, 30 feet high can easily be stretched and painted. Also at the south side of the theatre are five stories of rooms, approached by a convenient staircase, including the green-room, a fire-proof room for the wardrobe of the theatre, the "star" apartments, and about thirty dressing rooms — comfortably appointed in all respects. The green-room is a spacious and handsome parlor, on the second floor, the walls of which are adorned with theatrical engravings. From the vaults beneath the stage run passages conducting into the vaults beneath the auditorium, and also into those beneath the contiguous sidewalks. As the visitor roams through these strange caverns he is impressed anew with a sense of the solidity of this splendid structure. Here is seen the foundation, which is of solid rock. Here are the supports — stone pillars, nearly three feet square. The front wall is nearly five feet thick, and the thickness of the other walls is upwards of two feet. Under the sidewalk in Twenty-Third Street, is the carpenters' shop of the theatre, in a large, dry vault; and under the sidewalk in Sixth Avenue are two large boilers which supply steam for an engine, and for the hot-air pipes by which the theatre is heated. These boilers, it is understood, have been well tested, and declared to be perfectly safe. There are tanks of water at the top of the building.   Rope is not used on the stage, its place being supplied by wire cable.

These details suggest something like an adequate idea of the massiveness and beauty of Booth's Theatre.   It is a worthy monument of noble enterprise. It adorns the architecture of a great city.   It rewards industry and encourages art.   It diffuses a pure moral and intellectual influence.   And, in its stately strength of aspect and unsullied grace of character, it typifies at once the dignity of the art of acting and the esteem in which the drama is held by the educated community of the chief city of the American Republic.

The new house was completed in January, 1867.   Booth had employed the interim between the burning of the Winter Garden and the opening of his new theatre in professional labor about the country.   One of the first cities that he visited was Chicago; and there, in the Fall of 1867, he met, and was betrothed to, Miss Mary McVicker, who is now his wife.   He had first seen her in 1858, when she was but nine years old, and when she attracted his attention as a prodigy of precocious talent.   Her powers as a vocalist were, in particular, very remarkable in one so young.   She sang in concerts with Signor Brignoli; and upon the dramatic stage she acted juvenile parts — such as *Eva*, in "Uncle Tom's Cabin" — with cleverness, and to the approbation of the public.   Seeing her after a lapse of nine years, Booth found her matured by time and polished by education, keenly intelligent in mind, sanguine in temperament, joyously vivacious, and endowed with both the sense and the faculty of sparkling humor.   The effect of such an individuality, acting, through the affections, on a repressed, self-questioning, mournful nature, may readily be surmised.   Original, bright, quaint, and gleesome, she came like a gleam of spring sunshine upon the darkened life of the lonely and gloomy tragedian.   At his request — when he acted at McVicker's Theatre, in Chicago, in 1867 — this lady returned to the stage, playing *Ophelia*, to the actor's *Hamlet;* and subsequently, during this and other engagements, there and elsewhere, she coöperated with him in various of the chief female characters in the drama.   At a later period she accompanied him to New York; and, on the opening night of the new theatre, she acted *Juliet* to Booth's *Romeo*. Their marriage took place at Long Branch, New Jersey, on the 7th of June, 1869.   Miss McVicker's last professional appearance was made at Booth's Theatre, in the spring of that year, as *Desdemona*.   Mrs. Booth retired at once from the stage; with no purpose of ever resuming its pursuit.

The opening of Booth's Theatre, on the 3rd of February, 1869, was the most important dramatic event that had fixed the attention of the metropolis for several years, and it was viewed with lively interest and thoughtful consideration. The day had been stormy and the night was unpleasant, but the auditorium of the new theatre was crowded with a brilliant company. "Hail Columbia" — our nearest approach to a National Anthem — was performed by Mr. Edward Mollenhauer and his band, and then, responding to the public call, Booth came forward and addressed the assembly :

"Before the curtain rises on our play," he said, "let me bid you a welcome, warm as heart can make it, to my new theatre. It has long been my desire to build a theatre that might be regarded as worthy of our great metropolis; and at last my ambition is realized, and, by the kind coöperation of my valued friend, Mr. Richard A. Robertson, I am enabled to offer this one. I should, however, be unworthy of this success did I now fail to acknowledge the unvarying kindness wherewith the public of New York has cheered me on my professional pathway. For two years I have been absent from you ; and in that time I have worked very hard, and endured much anxiety — as was naturally the case, with such an enterprise as this upon my hands. But now I have returned, once more I trust to enjoy your favor. When the Winter Garden was burned, I had been announced to play *Romeo ;* and it has seemed to me fit that I should resume my professional labors before you precisely at the point where they were so abruptly ended. For such defects as may be noticeable in the working of the scenery to-night, I solicit your indulgence. Once more I sincerely thank you for your presence."

An opening address, in verse, written for this occasion by Mr. Edmund Falconer, of London, was circulated, in print, on the play-bills, but was not spoken. The opening performance — of "Romeo and Juliet" — was followed with eager attention, and, at various points, the pleasure of the vast assembly broke forth in delighted plaudits. Booth presented an original, carefully studied, and definite ideal of *Romeo*, very different from that which is usually offered. Its peculiarity was an uncommon fidelity to nature in preserving the callowness of the sentimental period of youth. The Veronese lover was made exceedingly boyish, until the explosive point in the third act, when *Romeo* avenges *Mercutio* by killing *Tybalt*. After that he was shown to be rapidly matured, under the pressure of calamity and grief. This view of Shakspeare's conception, though not received with unanimous approval, found, nevertheless, its ardent admirers. Another notable peculiarity of the performance was its presentation of the street-fight between the Montagues and the Capulets, with which, in Shakspeare, the action of the piece commences. The scenery employed was of a magnificence altogether unprecedented.

" Romeo and Juliet" ran for ten weeks, and earned upwards of sixty thousand dollars for the treasury of the new house.

Other and greater successes followed. " Othello" was brought out, with sumptuous appointments, on the 12th of April, and ran until the 29th of May. Booth acted *Othello.* It is one of his best works, conceived in an imaginative mood — so terribly earnest as almost to obscure the painfully offensive quality of the play. As an analysis and portrayal of the passion of jealousy, when that passion is aroused by suspicion of outrage against the affections and the sexual bond, " Othello" covers the whole ground, leaving nothing to be thought or said. As the embodiment of a harrowing and pathetic story, it overwhelms the mind with horror and the heart with anguish; as a study of human nature, it pierces to the lowest root of its subject, and delineates character and passion with a breadth of view and a firmness of touch that are nothing less than wonderful. As a work of constructive art it is perfect. All these points are clearer to the reader of the play than they possibly can be to the spectator of its representation. " Othello" is not played as Shakspeare wrote it — and no thinker, no man of taste, could wish to see it so played. Such a one must be aware that the poet has pursued his theme to every issue, sparing neither loathsome image nor foul word, nor ever veiling nor extenuating the unclean passions and hellish villainy that are his instruments. Even when toned down upon the stage, " Othello," through all the soft disguises, shows to the mental eye as the dissection of something excrescent and horrible — revealing the distinctly beastial side of human nature. Literature would be incomplete without it, though, and, for many reasons, no lover of the drama would desire to see it banished from the theatre. What should be claimed, however, as the right of sensibility and taste, is that a work so terrible and so painful shall not be lightly presented: and this claim was entirely satisfied in Booth's revival of the tragedy. It had forty-two successive representations, and, in closing its career, Booth closed his first engagement.

To comment on every incident that has attended the march of enterprise at the new theatre would probably be to increase the bulk without adding to the interest of this memoir; and the writer must, therefore, be content to tell the story of the house in a brief summary of events. Mr. Edwin Adams, who had acted *Mercutio* and *Iago,* in the two Shakspearean revivals that have been mentioned, succeeded Booth, on the 31st of May, and acted till the 31st of July — in " The Lady of Lyons," " Narcisse," " The Marble Heart," " Wild Oats," and " Enoch Arden." Jefferson, as *Rip Van Winkle* — that perfect exposition of lovely temperament, delicious humor, and imaginative and pathetic experience — appeared on the 2nd of August, and acted till the 18th of September. Miss Kate Bateman followed, and with twenty-four performances of *Leah*, and thirty-six of *Mary Warner*, carried the season on till the last of November. The first original play ever performed in the new theatre — Mr. Arthur Matthison's dramatization of "Enoch Arden" — was presented on the off-nights of this engagement. Hackett, as *Falstaff*, played from the 29th of November till December 25th. Mrs. Emma Waller came then, and strongly impressed the public by a very vigorous and pathetic embodiment of *Meg Merrilies*. On the 5th of January, 1870, Booth reappeared, in *Hamlet* — the stage accessories, on this occasion, being grander and finer than any ever before used in this country, in the presentation of this tragedy — and he continued to play the part in which he is most famous, and most worthy of fame, till the 19th of March. He was subsequently seen as *Sir Giles, Claude Melnotte*, and *Macbeth* — the latter personation being offered on the 28th of March. Mr. John S. Clarke, as *De Boots* and *Toodles*, commenced an engagement on the 18th of April, and, subsequently appearing as *Bob Tyke, Babington Jones, Gosling*, and *Tom Tackle*, he remained till the 28th of May. Mr. J. H. McVicker, in Mr. Charles Gayler's comedy of "Taking the Chances," then filled a short engagement. The play of "The Huguenot" was brought forward on the 14th of June, and kept on the stage till the 4th of July, when the theatre was closed. It reopened on the 15th of August, when Jefferson once more — and this time for a period of five months — delighted the public with his matchless impersonation of *Rip Van Winkle*. He acted the part one hundred and forty-nine times in succession, and his engagement extended till the 7th of January, 1871; on the 9th, Booth reappeared as *Richelieu* — the drama being revived with such splendor of scenes and dresses as not even this theatre, renowned for richness and beauty of stage embellishments, had before displayed to public view. "Richelieu" was kept on the stage eight weeks, and had forty-eight representations. On the 6th of March, Booth produced "Much Ado about Nothing," and appeared, for the first time in New York, as *Benedick*. Fourteen performances were given, and it was then succeeded, on the 20th of March, by "Othello" — Booth acting the *Moor* and Mr. Lawrence Barrett *Iago*. A revival of "The Fool's Revenge" took place on the 3rd of April, and Booth once more enacted *Bertuccio*. On the 24th of April, "A Winter's Tale" was brought out, with Mr. Barrett as *Leontes*. The stage-setting of this piece was a marvel of loveliness. It ran till the 3rd of June. On the 5th, Mr. W. G. Wills's beautiful play of "The Man of Airlie" was acted, with Mr. Barrett as *James Harebell;* and this — a rich and permanent addition to the literature of the stage — was performed till the close of the theatrical year, and the closing of the house, on the 4th of July. A new theatrical year began on the 14th of August, when Miss Lotta was brought forward in Mr. John Brougham's drama of "Little Nell," based on the "Old Curiosity Shop" of Dickens. Her series of performances extended till the 25th of September. Miss Charlotte Cushman, returning to the stage after ten years of retirement — a retirement which, it was thought would be final, but from which the illustrious actress emerged in all the stateliness and intellectual fire of other days — then commenced an engagement, as *Queen Katharine*, in Shakspeare's "Henry VIII." Mr. William Creswick, of London, likewise appeared, at this time, as *Cardinal Wolsey*. These artists have since been seen in the tragedy of "Macbeth;" and Miss Cushman has thrilled the public heart with her wonderful embodiment of *Meg Merrilies*. Mr. John E. Owens appeared, as *Caleb Plummer*, on the 6th of November. This array of facts and dates, which it would be easy to embellish and illustrate, has, perhaps, a somewhat barren aspect as thus presented; but, to all persons familiar with the condition and resources of dramatic art in America, it will have a great and worthy significance. It shows, on the part of Edwin Booth, a conscientious sense of those grave obligations to public morality and the cause of education which rest on the theatrical manager: it shows that the affairs of his theatre have been conducted in a steadfast spirit of sympathy with what is pure and good in the substance and the influence of dramatic art: and therein it shows that he has fairly earned — what he so fully enjoys — the respect of all intellectual workers, and the gratitude and admiration of the public. Within the current year Booth has purchased his partner's interest in the theatre, and has thus become its sole proprietor.

A number of miscellaneous facts, with reference to the Booth family, may be deemed germane to this narrative, and are, therefore, allotted a brief paragraph in this place. Junius Brutus Booth, the father of the tragedian, whose career is herein sketched, was born at St. Pancras, near London, in 1796. His father was a lawyer. His mother was a descendant of the famous John Wilkes, whose wit and audacity proved so vexatious to the Government of England in the days of George the Third. In early life Junius seems to have been what Longfellow somewhere describes as a "miscellaneous youth and a universal genius." He showed some talent for painting. He entered into the service of the British Navy. He learned the printer's art, and dabbled in literature. Then he became a sculptor. At last he found his true vocation and adopted the profession of the stage. His debut was made at Deptford, in England, on the 13th of December, 1813, when he acted *Campillo*, in Tobin's comedy of "The Honeymoon." His first appearance in London was made in 1815, as *Sylvius*, in "As You Like It." A little later he made a great hit, at Brighton, as *Sir Giles Overreach.* On the 12th of February, 1817, he played at Covent Garden, as *Richard III.*, and won a triumphant success against determined prejudice and bitter opposition. In 1820 he was married to Miss Holmes, of Reading, England, who accompanied him to America, in the summer of 1821. His first professional appearance in this country was made on the 13th of July, in that year, at Richmond, Virginia, as *Richard III.* He then came to the old Park Theatre, New York, where he made a marked and valuable impression ; and this he deepened by playing successful engagements all over the Union. One result of this prosperity was the acquisition of a farm, near Baltimore, in Maryland, which he kept all his life, and which is now the property of his widow and two of their children, Junius and Rosalie. After his first tour of the States he made a visit to England, but found no encouragement to remain there, and came back in 1824. America always appreciated his genius and always treated him with honor and kindness. His last appearance in the North was made at the new National Theatre, in New York, September 19th, 1851, when he acted *Sir Edward Mortimer* and *Shylock.* The circumstances concerning his trip to California, and his death, on the homeward passage, have already been related.

A thorough, able, and delightful study of the acting of this illustrious artist has been made by Mr. Thomas E. Gould, under the title of "The Tragedian." "In person," says this narrative, "Mr. Booth was short, spare, and muscular ; with a head and face of antique beauty ; dark hair ; blue eyes ; a neck and chest of ample but symmetrical mould ; a step and movement elastic, assured, kingly. His face was pale, with that healthy pallor which is one sign of a magnetic brain. Throughout this brief, close-knit, imperial figure, nature had planted and diffused her most vital organic forces ; and made it the capable servant of the commanding mind that descended into and possessed it in every fibre." Of his art, the same writer says : "Nature was the deep source of his power ; and she imparted her own perpetual freshness to his personations. We could not tire of him, any more than we tire of her. His art was, in a high sense, as natural as the bend of Niagara ; as the poise and drift of summer clouds ; the play of lightning ; the play of children ; or as the sea, storm tossed, sunlit, moonlit, or brooded in mysterious calm — and his art awakened in the observer corresponding emotions."

The family of Junius Brutus Booth comprised ten children : Junius Brutus ; Rosalie Anne ; Henry Byron ; Mary ; Frederick ; Elizabeth ; Edwin ; Asia Sydney ;

John Wilkes; and Joseph Addison. Five are dead. The survivors are Junius, Rosalie, Edwin, Asia (Mrs. J. S. Clarke), and Joseph. The middle name of Forrest has been incorrectly ascribed to Edwin. His middle name is Thomas; but he has never used it excepting upon legal documents.

Enough has been set down, in this sketch, to fulfill a portion of its promise and give its reader a distinct outline, at least, of Edwin Booth's personal and professional career. To fill in that outline — to make it an ample, thorough, minute narrative, permeated with the *life* of the actor — would be to occupy a larger space than has here been placed at the writer's disposal, and to produce a more pretentious and formidable work than the importance of the subject might now seem to justify. With the facts and opinions here stated, and with the twelve character-portraits of Booth, which this text has been prepared to accompany, the reader possesses what, it is hoped, will prove a satisfactory memorial of one of the most admired actors of the age.

In what is here written, the purpose has been — as in biography it should always be — to manifest the subject, and not the views and feelings of the writer. This purpose has enjoined the use of carefully tempered language, and has likewise enforced a considerable repression of personal enthusiasm. So much, in the character and in the acting of Edwin Booth is gentle, delicate, winning, and admirable, that affectionate appreciation of him, uncurbed by reserve, might chance to utter itself in extravagant terms, and thus misrepresent its object. There can be no invalid pretension, however, in claiming for him — what the facts of his career and the achievements of his art and labor clearly show him to possess — a mind animated by noble purpose, a worthy ambition controlled and directed by keen sense of moral integrity, and a spirit spontaneously chivalric in the conduct of life.

Edwin Booth is not yet forty years of age, and he has labored only about twenty years in the vocation of acting: yet he has established the most magnificent theatre in America, and he has attained, in the esteem of his countrymen in all parts of the Republic, the high and honorable rank of the representative tragedian of the time. Success of this kind is the result of neither luck nor accident. Favorable circumstances may, indeed, have accelerated its attainment; but they never could have placed within the grasp of a poor-minded and unworthy man the gracious and pure reward of the sincere devotion of genuine ability to the service of a great art.

That reward comes only to men of a high order of intellect, coupled with indomitable energy, severe patience, and that innate consciousness of real power and honest motive which sustains the mind through trouble, toil, neglect, temporary failure, disappointment, dejection, the desolate sense of bereavement, the perplexing annoyances of care, the acute knowledge of being misunderstood and misrepresented, the insolence of envy, and the venomous slanders of sleepless malice. All these Edwin Booth has had to encounter; and over them all — and in despite of hereditary peculiarities most inimical and dangerous to symmetry of character and happiness of life — he has risen into triumph : the triumph of upright and beneficent conduct and illustrious reputation. This result, the warrant for this humble memorial, is justly ascribed to the force of natural talents, tireless industry, impressive moral worth, sincerity, attractive individuality, and, over all, the glamour of genius —

> " The untaught strain
> That sheds beauty on the rose."

Upon the scope and qualities of that genius it seems impossible that remark should take the form of absolute precision. The dreamy odor of the jasmine is not more illusive than is the secret of that magnetic charm which at once enkindles and hallows the intellect, making it potent to beguile mankind of equal admiration and love. Spiritual essence seems always to baffle words. A human soul is not to be described as if it were a field of turnips. In the endless study of dramatic criticism, moreover, the results of analysis can never be irrefragibly authentic nor generally acceptable. To comprehend — amply and minutely — an actor's ideal of an author's conception, and to compare that ideal with one's own, approving if it corresponds and disapproving if it differs (with due concession for knowledge imparted, and due revision of instructed opinion), is,. of course, the obvious, fair, and usual method. Yet it seldom leads a student to unqualified admiration. of all the works of an actor, and it often leaves critics, of liberal culture and competent judgment, in the attitude of wide dissent from one another's conclusions.

Without assuming, however, to state the exact elements of the genius by which Booth's impersonations are illumined, it may be suggested that its salient attributes are imagination, intuitive insight, spontaneous grace, intense emotional fervor, and melancholy refinement. In his great works — in *Hamlet, Richelieu, Othello, Iago, Bertuccio,* and *Lucius Brutus* — these are conspicuously manifest. But perhaps, the controlling attribute, the one which imparts individual character, color, and fascination to his acting, is the gently thoughtful, introspective habit of a stately mind, abstracted from passion and toned by mournful dreaminess of temperament. The moment this charm begins to work, his victory as an artist is

complete.   It is this that makes him the veritable image of Shakspeare's thought,
in the glittering halls of Elsinore, on its mid-night battlements, and in its lonesome,
wind-beaten place of graves.   It is at once the token and the limit, if not of
his power most certainly of his magic.

He has, it is true, shown remarkable versatility.   He can pass with ease
from the boisterous levity of *Petruchio* to the height of *Hamlet's* sublime delirium
on the awful confines of another world.   *Othello*, the Moor, *Iago*, the Venetian,
Richelieu, the French priest, and *Don Cæsar*, the Spanish gallant — emblems of a
great variety of human nature and experience — are all, as he presents them,
entirely distinct individuals.   But all the results of his versatility are not in-
variably good.   Some of them lack the form of truth, and some of them lack
the touch of sympathy.

His *Richard III.*, for instance, though full of fire and marvelously effec-
tive at points, leaves in the critical mind a sense of incompleteness.   It is somewhat as though an artist, who should have cut a marble statue, had painted a
picture instead.

In Shakspeare, the character of *Richard* is that worst of monstrous creations —
a wicked man of genius.   The ugliness of his soul is symbolized in the ugliness
of his body.   Bitter, fiery, arrogant, cruel, impelled by devilish energy which
never halts nor flags, he is determined to rule a world which hates him.   His
intellect is towering and royal.   He looks down upon human passions and
makes them his playthings.   He uses all men and trusts none.   He is alone —
and he walks alone, along his bloody path to imperial power.   He knows himself,
too, and is never cajoled.   His hypocrisy may deceive others but it does not
deceive him.   He can take on all moods at will, and can secretly exult over
the duplicity of each.   He is the wit, the courtier, the lover, the man of the
world, the boon companion, the soldier, the statesman, and the king.   Within
the black silence of his own soul his genius sits and broods, like a scoffing
demon.   One little spark of human weakness there is somewhere within him, and
through that the all-powerful and ever-watchful Nemesis strikes him at last.   During
the earlier and larger part of his career, not Niagara itself is more steadfast in
its course than is the current of his tremendous and hellish will.   But at last
a mother's curse smites him, through crown and sceptre and royal robes, and
from that moment his genius begins to wither.   His crimes come back upon him.
Fear — a new phantom, more hideous than all the rest — appals his soul ; and he
rushes, in fiend-like fury, to a desperate and bloody death.

Booth's embodiment of the part suggests all this.   Its whole carriage is superb. Its emotion has the play of the lightning. Its subtle irony and heaven-defying audacity are, beyond description, true and fine. But, back of all, there is a certain fine tone of humane sensibility, a reservation of sweetness, which colors the whole work and defeats its earnestness. It has a thousand beauties — but it is not utterly hateful. The same peculiarity — an evanescent, gossamer-like suggestion of innate goodness — is present in his personation of *Iago*, the best of all the stage-villains he has ever depicted. But there its presence is a merit — two-thirds of a true embodiment of *Iago* being the simulation of the most winning integrity. Besides, the basis of the character is spiritualized intellect, perverted to the service of hell instead of being hallowed to the cause of heaven.

Under the discipline of sorrow, and through "years that bring the philosophic mind," Booth, like all true artists, drifts further and further away from what is dark and terrible, whether in the possibilities of human life or in the ideal world of imagination. It is the direction of true growth: it is the advance of original individuality: it is the sign of happy promise. In all characters that evoke the essential spirit of the man — in all characters, that is, which rest on the basis of spiritualized intellect, or on that of sensibility to fragile loveliness, the joy that is unattainable, the glory that fades, and the beauty that perishes — he is easily peerless. Hamlet, Faust, Manfred, Jacques, Edgar of Ravenswood, Esmond, Sydney Carton, Clifford Pyncheon, and Sir Edward Mortimer are all — in different ways — typical or suggestive of the personality that Edwin Booth has been destined to illustrate. It is the loftiest type of personality that life affords, because it is the embodied supremacy of the soul over the body, and because therein it denotes the only possible escape from the cares and vanities of a vanishing world.

" Thou hast been

As one, in suffering all, that suffers nothing :
A man, that fortune's buffets and rewards
Hast ta'en with equal thanks : and blest are those
Whose blood and judgment are so well commingled
That they are not a pipe for fortune's finger
To sound what stop she please : give me that man
That is not passion's slave, and I will wear him
In my heart's core, ay, in my heart of heart,
As I do thee. "

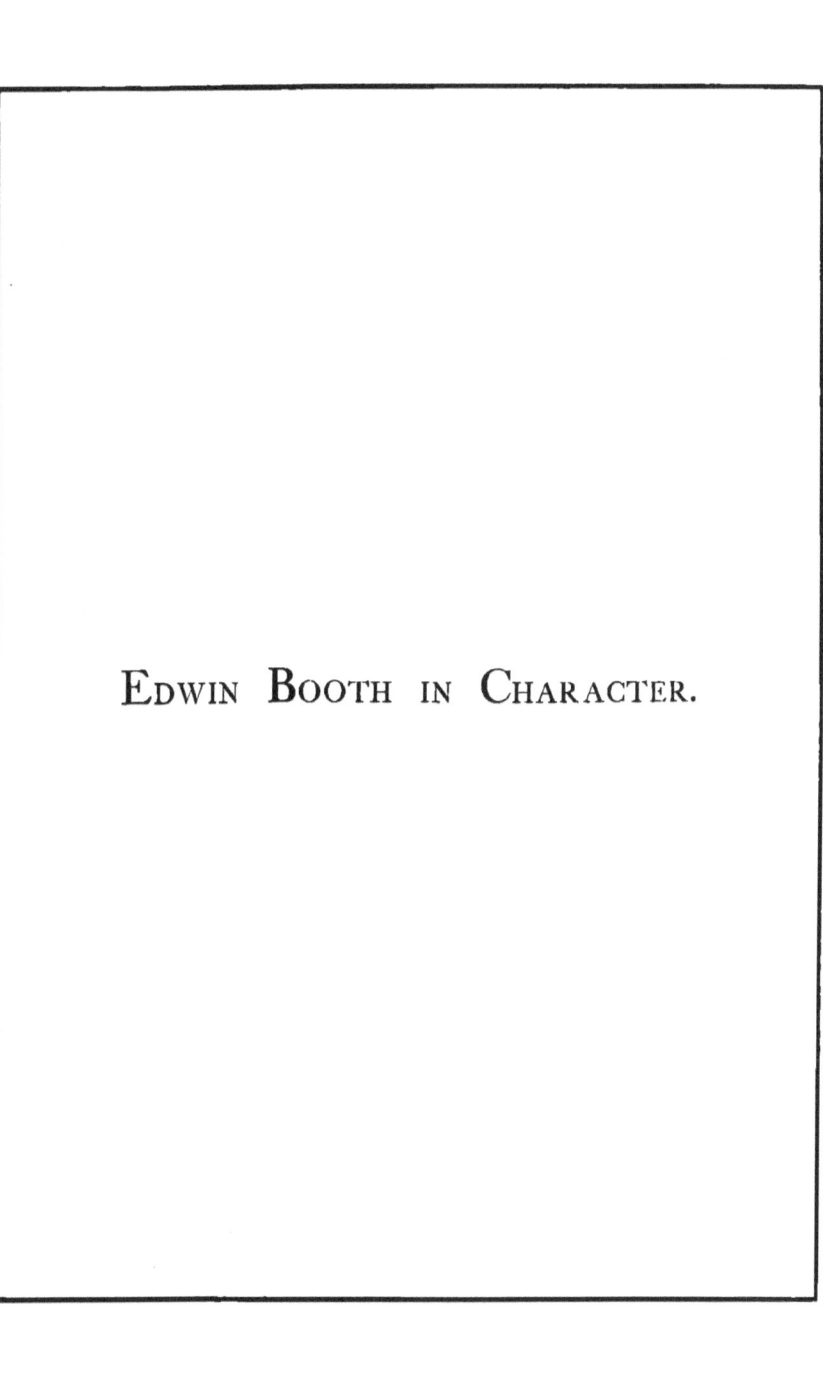

EDWIN BOOTH IN CHARACTER.

HAMLET.

The Churchyard.

———

HAMLET : That skull had a tongue in it and could sing once : How the knave jowls it
to the ground, as if it were Cain's jaw-bone, that did the first murder ! This might be
the pate of a politician, which this ass now o'er-reaches : one that would circumvent
God, might it not ?

HORATIO : It might, my lord.

HAMLET : Or of a courtier, which would say, *Good morrow, sweet lord !* *How dost thou, good
lord ?* This might be my lord such-a-one, that praised my lord such-a-one's horse, when
he meant to beg it : might it not ?

HORATIO : Ay, my lord.

HAMLET : Why, e'en so : and now my lady Worms : chapless and knocked about the mazzard
with a sexton's spade. Here's fine revolution, an' we had the trick to see 't. Did
these bones cost no more the breeding but to play at loggats with them ? Mine ache
to think on 't.

— *HAMLET. Act* v. *Scene* i.

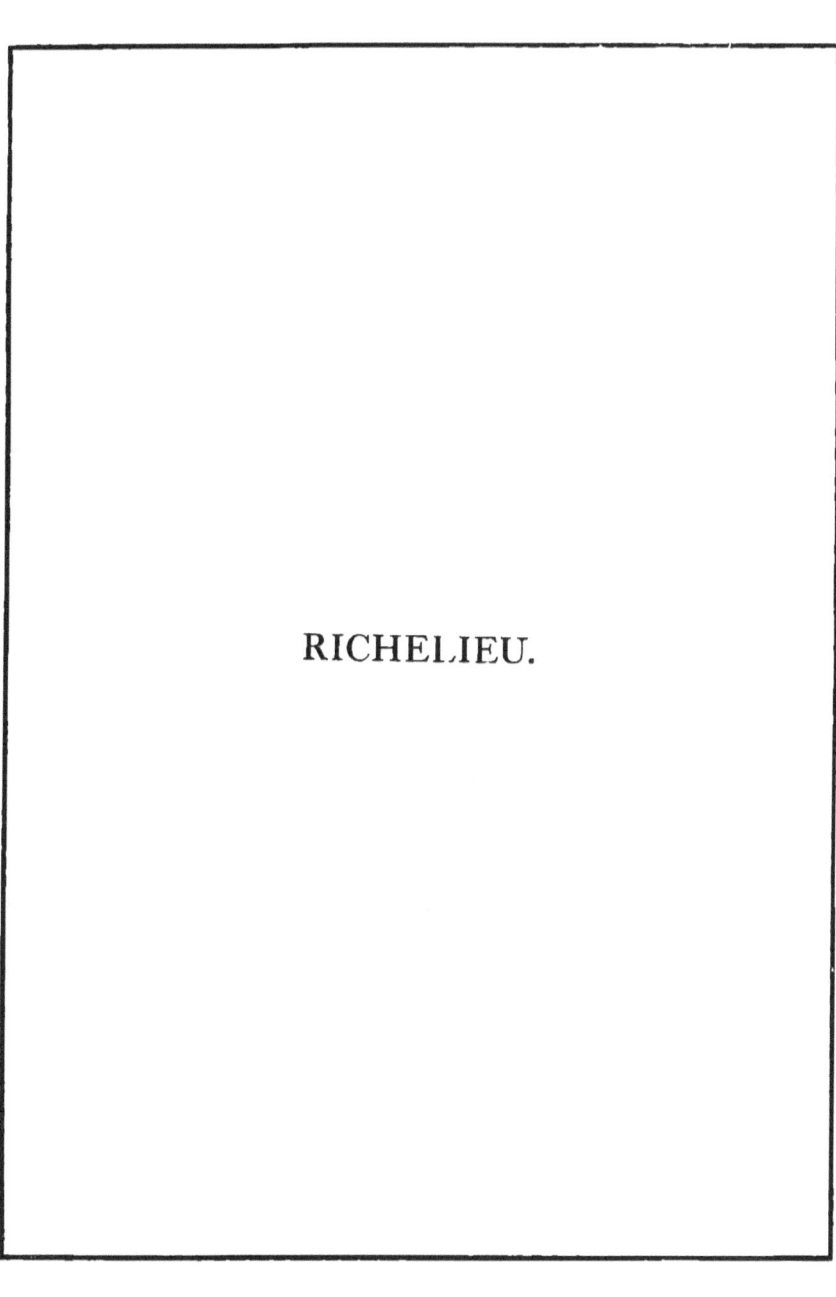

RICHELIEU.

The Garden of the Louvre.

BARRADAS : Seize him — disarm — to the Bastile !

[DE MAUPRAT *is seized. Enter* RICHELIEU, *attended by* JOSEPH *and his guard.*]

BARRADAS : The dead returned to life !

LOUIS : What ! a *mock* death ! This tops
The infinite of insult.

DE MAUPRAT : Priest and Hero ! for you are both —
Protect the truth !

RICHELIEU : What 's this ? (*Taking the writ.*)

DE BERINGHEN : Fact in philosophy : Foxes have got
Nine lives, as well as cats.

BARRADAS : Be firm, my liege.

LOUIS : I have assumed the sceptre — I will wield it.

JOSEPH : The tide runs counter — there 'll be shipwreck somewhere.

RICHELIEU : High treason ! — Faviaux ! — still that stale pretence.
My liege, bad men (ay, Count, most knavish men !)
Abuse your royal goodness. For this soldier,
France hath none braver — and his youth's hot folly,
Misled — (by whom *your Highness* may conjecture !) —
Is long since cancelled by a loyal manhood.
I, sire, have pardoned him.

LOUIS : And we do give your pardon to the winds !
Sir, do your duty !

RICHELIEU : What, sire ? you do not know — Oh, pardon me —
You know not yet, that this brave, honest heart
Stood between mine and murder ! Sire, for my sake —
For your old servant's sake — undo this wrong.
See, let me rend the sentence.

LOUIS : At your peril !
This is too much. Again, sir, do your duty !

RICHELIEU : Speak not, but go : — I would not see young Valor
So humbled as gray Service !

— RICHELIEU. Act iv. Scene i.

OTHELLO.

A Street in Venice.

———

OTHELLO: But look! What lights come yonder?

IAGO: These are the raiséd father and his friends:
  You were best go in.

OTHELLO: Not I: I must be found.
  My parts, my title and my perfect soul
  Shall manifest me rightly.
    *   *   *   *   *

RODERIGO: Signor, it is the Moor.

BRABANTIO: Down with him, thief!

IAGO: You, Roderigo! Come, sir, I am for you.

OTHELLO: Keep up your bright swords, for the dew will rust them.
  Good signor, you shall more command with years
  Than with your weapons.

BRABANTIO: * * Lay hold upon him: if he do resist,
  Subdue him at his peril.

OTHELLO: Hold your hands,
  Both you of my inclining and the rest.
  Were it my cue to fight, I should have known it
  Without a prompter.
                        — *OTHELLO. Act* i. *Scene* ii.

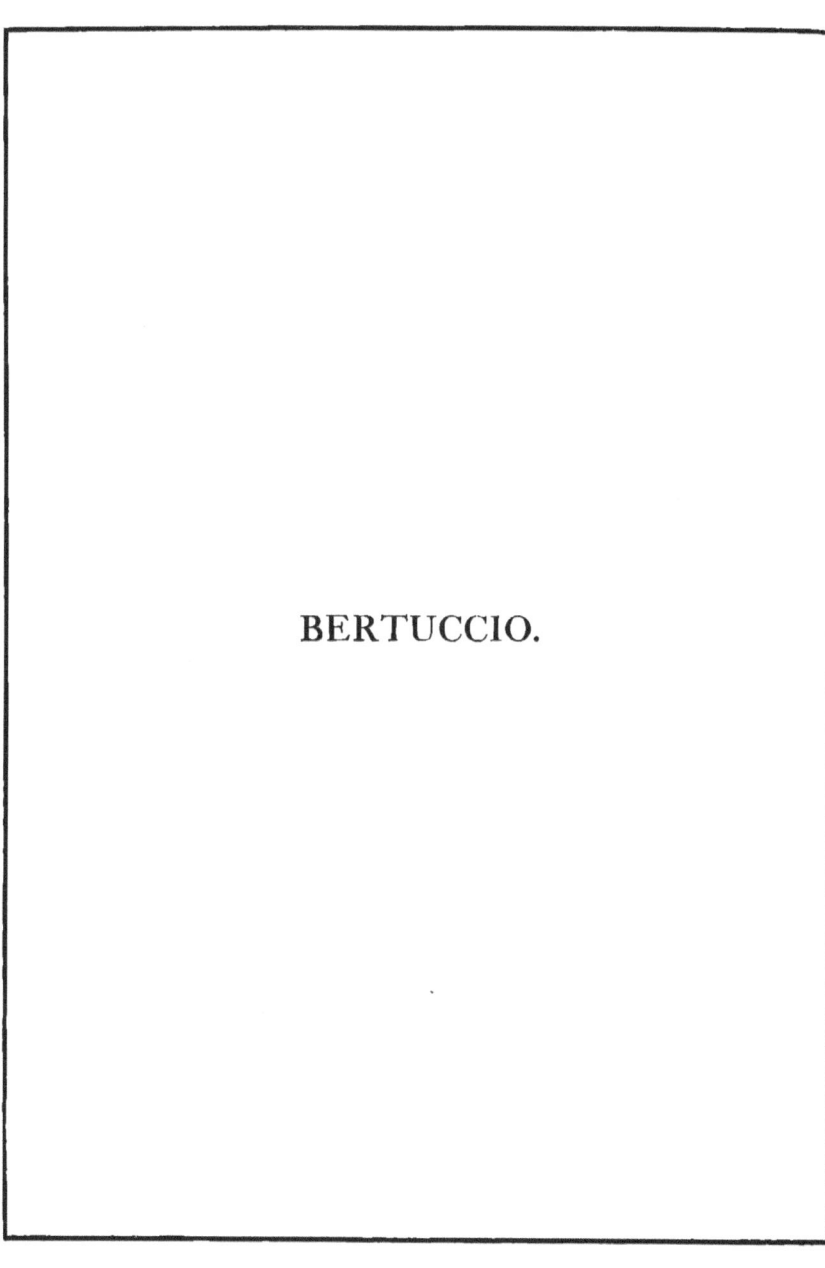

BERTUCCIO.

The Plotting of the Fool's Revenge.

BERTUCCIO : There 's a she-leopard
I lie and gaze at by the hour together :
So sleek, so graceful, and so dangerous,
I long to see her let loose on a man.
Trust me to draw the bolt and loose *my* leopard.
FRANCESCA : I 'll trust your love of mischief, not of me.
BERTUCCIO : That 's safest.
FRANCESCA : I must know how fares this fancy
Of Duke Manfredi for your pale Ginevra.
Mark him and her — their meetings — communings —
I know you 're private with my lord.
BERTUCCIO : He trusts me.
FRANCESCA : Here ! take my ring : your letters, sealed with this,
My page, Ascanio, will bring me straight.
'T is but three hours hard riding — and in six
I 'm here again. Mark ! write not on suspicion.
Let evil thought ripen to evil act.
That in the full flush of their guilty joys
I may strike sudden and strike home.
No Bentivoglio pardons.
BERTUCCIO : Have a care.
Faenza is Manfredi's ! . . . .
FRANCESCA : Give me my vengeance. Then come what may. . . . .

           (Exit Francesca.)

BERTUCCIO : (*Looking at the ring*) A blood-stone ! Apt reminder.
Does she think
That none but she has wrongs ? That none but she
Means to revenge them ? What ? "No Bentivoglio
Pardons." There is a certain vile Bertuccio ;
A twisted, withered, hunch-backed, court buffoon ;
A thing to make mirth, and to be made mirth of ;
A something betwixt ape and man, that claims
To hunt in couples with your ladyship.
You hunt Manfredi — I hunt Malatesta —
Let 's try which of the two has sharper fangs.

         — THE FOOL'S REVENGE. Act i. *Scene* i.

RICHARD III.

Bosworth Field.

———

KING RICHARD : Stir with the lark, to-morrow, gentle Norfolk.

NORFOLK · I warrant you, my lord.

KING RICHARD : Ratcliff —

RATCLIFF · My lord ?

KING RICHARD : Send out a pursuivant at arms
    To Stanley's regiment : bid him bring his power
    Before sun-rising, lest his son George fall
    Into the blind cave of eternal night. —
    Fill me a bowl of wine. — Give me a watch.
    (*To Catesby.*)   Saddle white Surrey for the field to-morrow.
    Look that my staves be sound, and not too heavy.
    Ratcliff —

RATCLIFF : My lord ?

KING RICHARD : Saw'st thou the melancholy Lord Northumberland ?

RATCLIFF . Thomas, the Earl of Surrey, and himself,
    Much about cock-shut time, from troop to troop,
    Went through the army, cheering up the soldiers.

KING RICHARD . I am satisfied. Give me a bowl of wine ;
    I have not that alacrity of spirit
    Nor cheer of mind that I was wont to have —
    So, set it down — Is ink and paper ready ?

RATCLIFF : It is, my lord.

KING RICHARD : Bid my guard watch ; leave me.
    About the mid of night, come to my tent
    And help to arm me. — Leave me, I say.

                     — *RICHARD III.*   *Act* v. *Scene* iii.

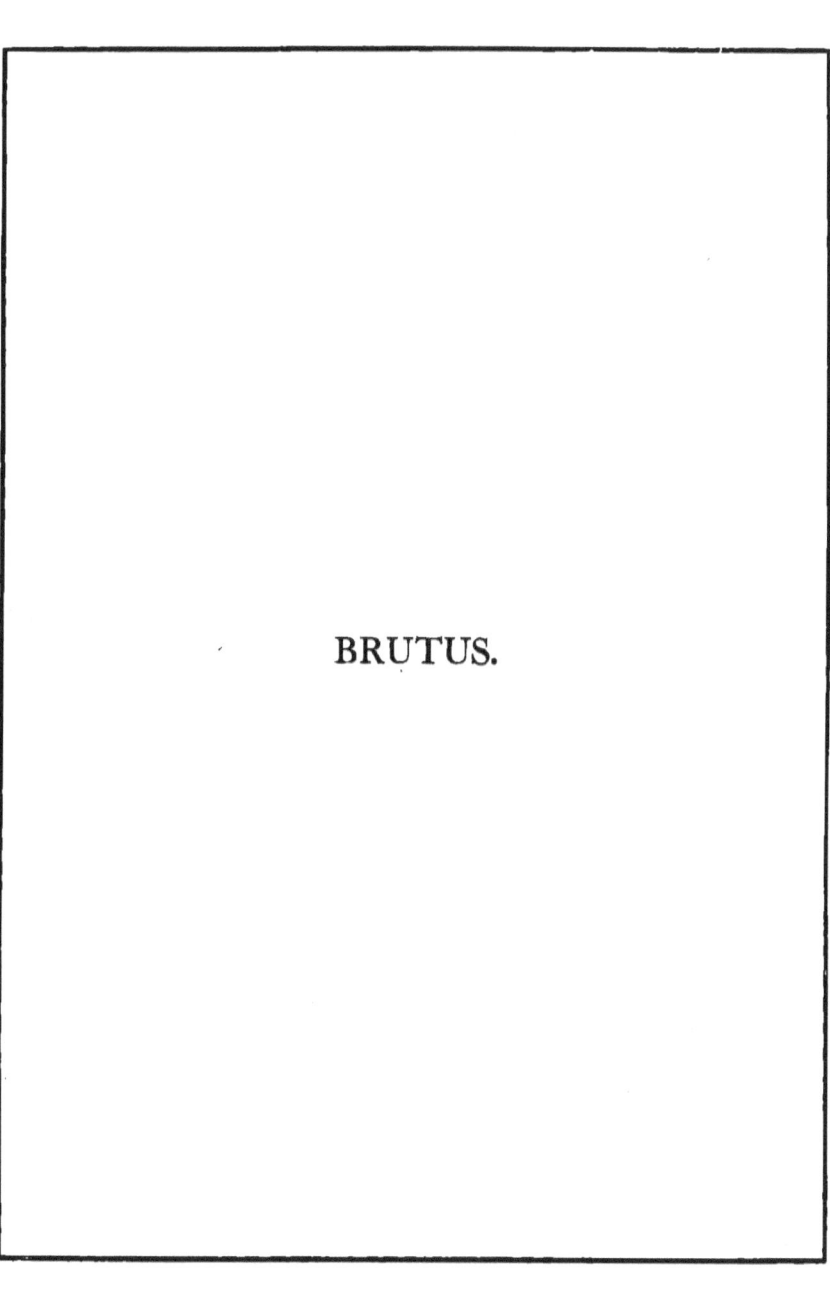

BRUTUS.

The Judgment.

BRUTUS * * Nay, Titus, more,
I must myself ascend yon sad tribunal,
And there behold thee meet this shame of death.
With all thy hopes and all thy youth upon thee. . . . .
TITUS : Die like a felon — ha, a common felon !
O Brutus, Brutus ! Must I call you father,
Yet have no token of your tenderness ? . . . .
How can I think that you did ever love me ?
BRUTUS : Think that I love thee by my present passion ;
By these unmanly tears, these earthquakes here,
These sighs that strain the very strings of life.
Let these convince you that no other cause
Could force a father thus to wrong his nature. . . . .
Embrace thy wretched father. May the gods
Arm thee with patience in this awful hour,
The sovereign magistrate of injured Rome
Condemns
A crime thy father's bleeding heart forgives.
Go, meet thy death with a more manly courage
Than grief now suffers me to show, in parting :
And, while she punishes, let Rome admire thee !
Farewell ! Eternally farewell ! . . . .
TITUS : Farewell forever.
BRUTUS : Forever. [*He ascends the Tribunal.*]
Lictors attend ! Conduct your prisoner forth.
VALERIUS : Whither ?
BRUTUS : To death ! When you do reach the spot,
My hand shall wave you signal for the act :
Then let the trumpet's sound proclaim it done.
[TITUS *is led out. A dead march is heard, slowly sinking into silence.* BRUTUS *alone.*]
Poor youth ! Thy pilgrimage is at an end.
A few sad steps have brought thee to the brink
Of that tremendous precipice whose depth
No thought of man can fathom. Justice now
Demands her victim. A little moment,
And I am childless. One effort, and 't is past.
[*He rises and waves his hand. Three sounds of the trumpet are heard.*]
Justice is satisfied and Rome is free.
[*He falls headlong from the Tribunal.*]
— *BRUTUS. Act* v. *Scene* iii.

KING LEAR.

The Heath — Night and Tempest.

LEAR : Blow wind, and crack your cheeks ! rage ! blow !
You cataracts, and hurricanoes, spout
Till you have drenched our steeples, drowned the cocks !
You sulphurous and thought-executing fires,
Vant couriers to oak-cleaving thunder-bolts,
Singe my white head ! And thou, all-shaking thunder,
Strike flat the thick rotundity o' the world !
Crack nature's moulds, all germens spill 'at once,
That make ingrateful man.

     *   *   *   *

I tax you not, you elements, with unkindness :
I never gave you kingdom, called you children :
You owe me no subscription ; why, then, let fall
Your horrible pleasure : here I stand, your slave,
A poor, infirm, weak, and despised old man : -
But I will call you servile ministers,
That have with two pernicious daughters joined
Your high-engendered battles 'gainst a head
So old and white as this.

     *   *   *   *

KENT : Good my lord, enter here.
LEAR : Wilt break my heart ?
KENT : I 'd rather break my own : Good my lord, enter.
LEAR : Thou think'st 'tis much, that this contentious storm
Invades us to the skin : so 'tis, to thee ;
But where the greater malady is fixed
The lesser is scarce felt. Thou'dst shun a bear
But, if thy flight lay toward the raging sea,
Thou'dst meet the bear i' the mouth. When the mind's free
The body's delicate : the tempest in my mind
Doth from my senses take all feeling else,
Save what beats there. — Filial ingratitude !
Is it not as this mouth should tear this hand
For lifting food to 't ? — But I will punish home : —
No, I will weep no more. — In such a night
To shut me out ! — Pour on : I will endure : —
In such a night as this ! O, Regan, Goneril ! —
Your old, kind father, whose frank heart gave all,
O, that way madness lies ; let me shun that ; —
No more of that.

                  — KING LEAR. Act iii. *Scenes* ii. *and* iv.

SHYLOCK.

A Street in Venice.

———

BASSANIO : This is Signor Antonio.

SHYLOCK : (*Aside.*) How like a fawning publican he looks !
    I hate him, for he is a Christian :
    But more, for that, in low simplicity,
    He lends out money, gratis, and brings down
    The rate of usance here with us in Venice.
    If I can catch him once upon the hip
    I will feed fat the ancient grudge I bear him.
    He hates our sacred nation ; and he rails,
    Even there, where merchants most do congregate,
    On me, my bargains, and my well-won thrift,
    Which he calls interest. Cursed be my tribe
    If I forgive him !

                — *MERCHANT OF VENICE. Act* i. *Scene* iii.

MACBETH.

The Cave of the Witches.

———

SECOND WITCH : By the pricking of my thumbs,
Something wicked this way comes. —
Open locks, whoever knocks.
    [*Enter* MACBETH.]
MACBETH : How now, you secret, black, and midnight hags,
What is 't you do ?
ALL : A deed without a name.
MACBETH : I conjure you by that which you profess
(Howe'er you came to know it), answer me :
Though you untie the winds and let them fight
Against the churches ; though the yesty waves,
Confound and swallow navigation up ;
Though bladed corn be lodged, and trees blown down ;
Though castles topple on their warders' heads,
Though palaces and pyramids do slope
Their heads to their foundations ; though the treasure
Of nature's germens tumble all together,
Even till destruction sickens, answer me
To what I ask you.
FIRST WITCH : Speak.
SECOND WITCH : Demand.
THIRD WITCH : We 'll answer.

                    — *MACBETH. Act* iv. *Scene* i.

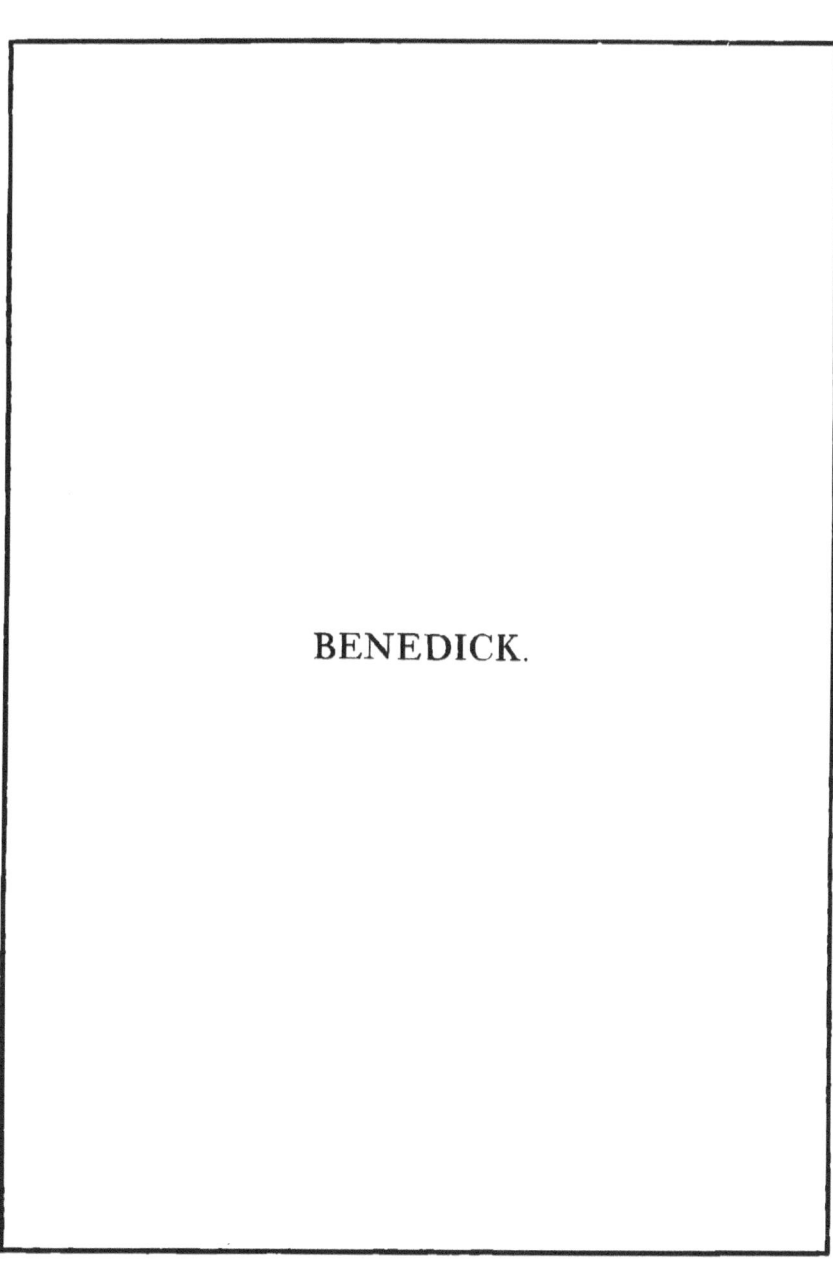

BENEDICK.

Leonato's Palace — Messina.

———

BENEDICK : Gallants, I am not as I have been.

LEONATO : So say I: methinks you are sadder.

CLAUDIO : I hope he be in love.

DON PEDRO : Hang him, truant ! There's no true drop of blood in him, to be truly touched with love : if he be sad, he wants money.

BENEDICK : I have the toothache.

DON PEDRO : Draw it.

BENEDICK : Hang it.

CLAUDIO : You must hang it first, and draw it afterwards.

DON PEDRO : What ? Sigh for the toothache ?

LEONATO : Where is but a humor or a worm.

BENEDICK : Well, every one can master a grief but he that has it.

— *MUCH ADO ABOUT NOTHING.* Act iii. *Scene* ii.

DON CÆSAR DE BAZAN.

The Ruined Cavalier.

—

Don Jose: As I live, 'tis Don Cæsar de Bazan—my old college friend at Salamanca.

Don Cæsar: (*Feeling his pockets*) Not a maravedi! By the aid of the dice-box, the rogues have cleaned me out as though they had been noblemen and men of honor. I must now trust to the air and the sky for board and lodging: Well—my supper will be light and my room airy.

Don Jose: Am I mistaken in addressing you as Don Cæsar de Bazan?

Don Cæsar: Eh! No, signor. What, Don Jose de Santarem?

Don Jose: The same.

Don Cæsar: (*Aside.*) His doublet is of three pile velvet.—What can he want with me?

Don Jose: When last we met you were young and prosperous.

Don Cæsar: Ah! You perceive the alteration (*Looks at his dress*). But I was always fond of change.

Don Jose: You inherited a noble name and a princely fortune.

Don Cæsar: True: I've preserved the one and spent the other. Is my name of any service to you?

Don Jose: I thank you, no. I had hoped you would have done great things, Don Cæsar.

Don Cæsar: So I have. If you doubt me, ask my creditors.

Don Jose: I thought your father paid your debts, when you quitted Salamanca.

Don Cæsar: So he did, worthy soul! so he did. But then, from the force of habit, I acquired new ones.

Don Jose: You have paid somewhat dearly for a life of pleasure.

Don Cæsar: Possibly: though I have freed myself now from all anxieties. I've no money, so I am not teased by poor relations. I've no lands, so am without a grumbling tenantry. I've no particular destination, so never take a wrong turning. I've nothing to support but my sword—and that keeps a sharp look out for itself.

—DON CÆSAR DE BAZAN. Act i. Scene i.

CLAUDE MELNOTTE.

The Interrupted Betrothal.

MELNOTTE: Her voice again ! How the old time comes o'er me !

*   *   *   *

PAULINE: Thrice have I sought to speak ; my courage fails me.
Sir, is it true that you have known—nay, are you
The friend of—Melnotte ?

MELNOTTE. Lady, yes ; myself
And misery know the man.

PAULINE: And you will see him,
And you will bear to him—ay, word for word,
All that this heart, which breaks in parting from him,
Would send, ere still for ever ?

MELNOTTE: He hath told me
You have the right to choose from out the world
A worthier bridegroom. He foregoes all claim,
Even to murmur at his doom. Speak on.

PAULINE: Tell him, for years I never nursed a thought
That was not his ; that on his wandering way,
Daily and nightly, poured a mourner's prayers.
Tell him, e'en now, that I would rather share
His lowliest lot ; walk by his side, an outcast ;
Work for him ; beg with him ; live upon the light
Of one kind smile from him ; than wear the crown
The Bourbon lost.

MELNOTTE: (Aside.) Am I already mad ?
And does delirium utter such sweet words
Into a dreamer's ear ? (Aloud.) You love him thus,
And yet desert him ?

PAULINE: Say that if his eye
Could read this heart—its struggles, its temptations—
His love itself would pardon that desertion !
Look on that poor old man—he is my father ;
He stands upon the verge of an abyss ;
He calls his child to save him ! Shall I shrink
From him who gave me birth ? Withhold my hand,
And see a parent perish ? Tell him this,
And say—that we shall meet again in heaven !

MELNOTTE: The night is past ! Joy cometh with the morrow !

—*THE LADY OF LYONS.*   *Act* v.   *Scene* iii.